MORE
Classic Classroom
Clangers

MORE
Classic Classroom
Clangers

VINCENT SHANLEY

**ROBSON
BOOKS**

First published in the United Kingdom in 2006 by
Robson Books
10 Southcombe Street
London
W14 0RA

An imprint of Anova Books Company Ltd

ISBN 9781861059574
A CIP catalogue record for this book is available from the
British Library.

10 9 8 7 6

Printed and bound by Creative Print and Design (Ebbw Vale),
Wales

This book can be ordered direct from the publisher.
Contact the marketing department, but try your bookshop first.

www.anovabooks.com

Contents

Foreword

Monday morning, for anyone who works and has recently enjoyed the pleasures of a weekend, represents purgatory. It is the start of the new week when duties and responsibilities can no longer be postponed and Friday seems a long way off. As a head teacher, each Monday morning I would highlight significant matters and events for the forthcoming week to a less than cheerful staff. Very rapidly the thought struck me that it might help to raise the odd chuckle and thereby engender a general feeling of well-being and goodwill if I included on the weekly bulletin a selection of amusing stories from the world of education. There were plenty of them from the school itself and the various educational bodies. In History, there had been the young lad from Year 8 who had written: 'Mozart was a child orgy . . .' and the Languages Department had guffawed with delight when a Year 11 student had looked up by mistake the wrong sort of 'piles' when translating 'piles of snow' in a French composition. And so, on delivery of the bulletin, while the teachers hardly fell about the staff-room floor clutching their stomachs in hilarity, it was pleasing to notice that the 'back page' became the first port of call. 'The Funnies' began, and offerings for inclusion flooded in.

From the Geography Department: Question: What is the best way to protect crops from storm? Answer: By planting trees. A sixty-foot tree can break wind from 300 yards.

From the R.E. Department: Moses came down from Mount Sinai with the tabloids.

From an overheard conversation: 'I wish I had her legs – on her they're such a waste.'

A parent's letter threw up this gem: 'Even though Jane left early for the bus, she had to come back with her stomach.'

Notices from other schools were contributed: 'Assistant Cook required for St Anselm's Junior School. (No objection to sex.)'

Teachers and head teachers were fair game because it was accepted that mistakes were a part of life, that we all drop clangers and we must learn to share in the joy of humour and self-deprecation. I myself announced in an assembly that an aged, now retired school governor had been 'killed in a road accident which had been fatal'.

This book is a sequel to Classic Classroom Clangers, *and I would like to thank all those teachers, grandparents, parents and friends who have passed onto me the material that has made* More Classic Classroom Clangers *possible.*

Vin Shanley, 2006

1

Setting the Scene

Mothers, quite literally, find children 'hard to bear' and look forward to the respite bedtime brings. Likewise, most grandparents love their grandchildren to bits but anticipate with glee those soothing words 'bye-bye'. Some people, of course, cannot abide anyone under twenty years of age and would echo the following sentiments.

I abominate the sight of them [children] so much that I have always had the greatest respect for the character of Herod. *(Lord Byron)*

I think children shouldn't be seen or heard. *(Jo Brand)*

Alligators have the right idea. They eat their young. *(Eve Arden)*

I love children, especially when they cry, for then someone takes them away. *(Nancy Mitford)*

W.C. Fields suggested to a friend who was having trouble with his daughter that he should 'throw her overboard'. When he received the response: 'You can't throw your own daughter overboard,' he replied, 'Why not? Let the sharks protect themselves.'

Those who are parents accept that there will be trials and tribulations on the path to adulthood (or 'adultery' as one young lad mistakenly called it) and know that those who protest along the lines of 'our children never caused us a moment's worry', are telling lies. Some are realistic or, perhaps, more cynical.

Money – the one thing that keeps us in touch with our children. *(Gyles Brandreth)*

I've got two wonderful children – and two out of five isn't bad. *(Henry Youngman)*

We all, of course, are aware that children can be rascals and challenging, and for that reason we can sympathise and empathise with the following situations and observations.

This is Miss Hambridge, our new schoolteacher. She's between nervous breakdowns. *(The Moon's Our Home)*

Noel Coward once attended a dreary play written around a fourteen-year-old so-called 'prodigy', who was on stage for most of the piece. 'Two things should have been cut,' Coward remarked. 'The second act and that youngster's throat.'

'Once when I was lost, I saw a policeman and asked him to help me find my parents,' Rodney Dangerfield recalled. 'I said, "Do you think we'll ever find them?" He said, "I don't know, kid. There are so many places they can hide."'

Never raise your hands to your kids – you leave your groin unprotected. *(Anon)*

Be nice to your kids – they will choose your nursing home. *(Anon)*

Having one child makes you a parent; having two makes you a referee. *(David Frost)*

However, love them or loathe them, one of their greatest attractions is the mirth and merriment they create with their 'bloopers' or 'gaffes'. We laugh not at them, but with them, because these 'clangers' are the result of their innocence, enthusiasm and their striving to learn and perfect their mother tongue. Very often they bring a level-headedness and realism to a situation hitherto unperceived. There is an abundance of common sense in the following answers.

Teacher: What was the first thing your mother said to you this morning?

Pupil: She said, 'where am I, Cathy?'

Teacher: And why did that upset you?

Pupil: Because my name is Susan, Miss.

Teacher: ALL your responses MUST be oral, OK? Which school did you go to?

Pupil: Oral.

Teacher: What is your date of birth?

Pupil: 18 July

Teacher: What year?

Pupil: Every year, Miss.

Perchance the following mistakes could well be the fault of grownups' lack of clear enunciation.

Q: Name one book written by Thomas Hardy.
A: Tess of the Dormobiles.

'Dour' means a kind of help like in the hymn, 'O God Dour Helping Ages Past'.

Then we have the replies that are almost there; they have come within a whisker of making it.

Granny says alcohol will be the urination of my uncle Bobby.

I believe muggers, whether they are men or women, should be put behind bras.

But it is not, of course, only children who drop 'clangers'. All of us, whether we be high and mighty, rich or poor, famous or insignificant, powerful or feeble, have our moments of madness or bouts of pure ignorance when we perpetrate gaffes. Such television programmes as It'll Be All Right On The Night would seem to suggest that committing 'clangers' is in vogue and de rigueur. The sensible stance to take, something actors seem to have realised, is that we accept our lack of perfection and have the good grace and humility to laugh with others.

While much of the following material concentrates on pupils, let us not forget that head teachers can come out with statements that cause staff and pupils to hoot with hilarity – when they are not there, of course.

Whenever I open my mouth, some fool speaks. *(Said at assembly)*

In two words – impossible.

My deputy head has been depressed since he began working with me in 2001.

Parents themselves send in letters of excuse or explanation that are sometimes humorous and beyond belief.

Thomas couldn't do his homework last night because we had to worm the dog.

I am pleased to tell you that my husband, who was reported missing, is dead.

Please excuse my daughter for being late. Her broom wouldn't start so I had to send it back to Salem for repairs!

However, it cannot be denied that the more influential, self-satisfied, superior and conceited a person is, the more we enjoy them making a cock-up. George W. Bush obtained little sympathy when he declared: 'I have opinions of my own – strong opinions – but I don't always agree with them'; or former vice-President Dan Quayle, when he expressed the view: 'I was recently on a tour of Latin America, and the only regret I have was that I didn't study Latin harder at school so I could converse with those people.' Perhaps George W. inherited his problems of communication from his father, Bush Senior, who must have scared the wits out of his presidential challenger by announcing: 'I'll put my manhood up against his any time.'

Unfortunately for those in the public eye, their gaffes are likely to be recorded and shared, whereas we lesser mortals have only our friends or family to chortle with pleasure and satisfaction.

This year's hairstyle is called a 'shag' and our resident stylist is here to give our model one. *(Lorraine Kelly)*

Born in Italy, most of his fights have been in his native New York. *(Des Lynam)*

MINERS REFUSE TO WORK AFTER DEATH. *(Headline in Economic Review)*

Such gaffes from the media abound and, in recognition of this, the final sections of this book are dedicated to them. Meanwhile, it's the children's turn.

2

School Subjects – English

The wife of a duke is a ducky.

A 'buttress' is a woman who makes butter . . . or maybe a female butcher?

Bacon was the man who thought he was Shakespeare.

A relative pronoun is a family pronoun such as 'mother', 'brother', 'aunt'.

John Ridd was very kind to his sisters and other dumb animals.

Syntax is all the money collected in a church from those who have sinned.

The future of 'I give' is 'I take'.

The word 'trousers' is an uncommon noun because it is singular at the top and plural at the bottom.

A coroner is a man whose job it is to decide whether a person died a natural or a fatal death.

There are many eligible fish in the North Sea.

A sheep is mutton covered in wool.

A sure-footed animal is an animal that when it kicks, it doesn't miss.

A litre is a nest of young puppies.

'The Complete Angler' is another name for Euclid because he wrote all about angles.

Q: What is meant by the word 'mortgage'?
A: When people want their diseased relatives to be buried, they send them to the mortuary where they are mortgaged.

The feminine of manager is menagerie.

Q: Caesar's wife was above . . . (fill in the missing word}
A: Forty.

Quadrupeds are not singular – you can't have a horse with one leg.

The plural of penny is two-pence.

Masculine – man; feminine – woman; neuter – corpse.

Pope wrote principally in heroic cutlets.

Shakespeare wrote comedies, tragedies and hysterectomies.

Homer wrote the Oddity.

An abstract noun is something you can't see when you are looking at it — it can't be heard, touched, seen or smelled.

Virgil was a man who used to clean up churches.

The masculine of vixen is vicar.

The masculine of heroine is kipper.

The poem of the 'Forsaken Merman' made me very angry — to think that a woman could leave a poor helpless man to get his own meals.

Byron wrote epics and swam the Hellespont. In between he made love drastically.

The plural of spouse is spice.

The plural of forget-me-not is forget-us-nots.

A widower is the husband of a widow.

Transparent means something you can see through, for example, a keyhole.

A phlegmatic person is one who has chronic bronchitis.

Poetry is when every line begins with a capital letter.

Q: Use a sentence to make it clear that you understand the meaning of the word 'posterity'.
A: The cat leaped about then sat on its posterity.

The Press today is the mouth-organ of the people.

You cannot tell the gender of 'egg' until it is hatched.

A pessimist is a person who is never happy unless he is miserable and even then he is not pleased.

Her mother, being immortal, died.

A passive verb is when the subject is the sufferer, as 'I am loved'.

A crematorium is the French for a dairy.

A prospectus is a man who looks for gold.

Pineapples come from pine trees.

Miguel Cervantes wrote 'Donkey Hote'.

Before becoming captain he had been an amiable seaman.

Dust is mud with the juice squeezed out.

A hostage is a lady who works in an airplane.

Teacher: Billy name two pronouns.
Billy: Who? Me?
Teacher: Well done.

Q: Which poet wrote all his poems in a synagogue?
A: Rabbi Burns.

The patchwork guilts had been sown by Grandma Dee.

Just trying to fill her shoes had been very difficult, but time will heel.

He was a rear image of his grandfather.

Children should be obscene and not heard.

He slipped into a comma and died.

We read three stories but the third one was the sadist.

He worked hard for under pillage children.

I looked everywhere to find an example of 'automat apia'.

The pleasures of youth are nothing to the pleasures of adultery.

Camelot represented the guarding of Edam.

Ernest Hemingway won the pull it surprise for his book *The Old Man and the Sea*.

At school she was involved in many extracellular activities.

It was a no hose barred meeting.

He took her for granite.

My father is retarded on a pension.

We have a tree in our garden suffering from Dutch realm disease.

Q: What do you understand by 'good manners'?
A: Good manners is the noise you don't make when you eat soup.

Q: What is half of infinity?
A: nity.

Q: What's a zebra?
A: 26 sizes larger than an 'A' bra.

ENGLISH PLUS

Threatening Letters – man asks for long sentence *(The Scotsman)*

I think Clueless was very deep. I think it was deep in the way that it was very light. I think lightness has to come from a very deep place if it's true lightness. *(Alicia Silverstone, star of the film* Clueless, *winning a Campaign For Plain English Award for talking complete rubbish)*

Richard Burton to teach English at Oforxd *(The Scotsman)*

Five thugs last night pulled the British passenger ship *Capetown Castle* clear of the sandbank at Flushing. *(Irish News & Belfast Morning News)*

Ken Bates was accused of being many things while he was chairman of Chelsea: arrogant, abrasive, evasive, cantankerous, ruthless, heartless, egotistical, greedy, secretive, self-serving and deluded. He also had his bad points. *(The Independent)*

An employee at the North-West Castle quoted Prince Philip's Secretary as saying the hotel for the peasant-hunting holiday starting November 25th was chosen on the toss of a coin. *(S.C.M. Post)*

The decision of the chairman, on any point, shall be fatal. *(Governors' minutes)*

The oddly gifted Hungarian painter to whom last week I compared the Belgian artist Spillaert was called Csontvary (1853–1919) and not Conservatory. *(Observer)*

Reading about the unfortunate stag hunted by the Devon and Somerset Staghounds last week reminded me of all the cruelty going on all over England to defenceless animals and children. I wish the law would tighten up and for every case of cruelty by these sadists give imprisonment and a severe lashing with the cat. *(Express & Echo)*

Conjugate the verb 'done great': I done great. You (s) done great. He, she or it done great. We done great. You (pl.) done great. They done great. The boy Lineker done great. *(Letter to Guardian on the World Cup commentating of Emlyn Hughes and Mike Channon)*

Eric: Who was that lady I seen you with last night?
Ernie: You mean, 'I saw'.
Eric: Sorry. Who was that eyesore I seen you with last night?

Bernard Shaw, who was in favour of rationalising the spelling of English, once commented: 'After all, if we were consistent we should spell fish "ghoti"; gh is pronounced like f in enough; o is pronounced like i in women; and ti is pronounced like sh in nation.'

The poet Robert Browning was asked by his future wife, Elizabeth Moulton-Barrett, what an exceptionally obscure passage in one of his poems meant. Having puzzled over the passage for some time, Browning gave up the struggle. 'Miss Barrett,' he said, 'when that passage was written only God and Robert Browning knew what it meant. Now only God knows.'

Albert Einstein was a very late talker. At the dinner table one evening, he finally broke his long silence: 'The soup is too hot,' he complained. His parents, greatly relieved, asked him why he had never spoken before. 'Because,' he replied, 'up to now everything has been in order.'

Dr Johnson once, in a fit of anger, felled a man with his own dictionary. Telling the story to a friend, the man concluded: 'He literally knocked me down.'

MISPRONUNCIATIONS, MISTAKES AND MISSPELLINGS

South E Sting-land = South East England

N H Chess = NHS

Stay colder pension schemes = Stake Holder Pension Schemes

Sick = six

Fith/sikth = fifth/sixth

Drawring = drawing

Unexpected surprise = surprise

Added bonus = bonus

Revert **back** = revert

Exit **out** = exit

Eggzit = exit

Irregardless = regardless

It went **badly** wrong = it went wrong

I was sat there = I was sitting there

Triathalon = triathlon

Decathalon = decathlon

Axed = asked

Ec-cetera = etcetera

Literally, as in: 'I literally froze to death.'

Proply = properly

I didn't do nothing = I didn't do anything

I would of come = I would have come

He done it = He did it

I seen him = I saw him

Where is your mother at? = Where is your mother?

He fell off of the chair = He fell off the chair

Vee-Hicle = vehicle

Ex-cape = escape

Jew-lary = jewellery

It ordipends = It all depends

Sec-er-tary = secretary

Asseptable = acceptable

You can't eat your cake and have it too = You can't have your cake and eat it.

Libary = library

Mash potatoes = mashed potatoes

Damp squid = damp squib

Cold slaw = cole slaw

Duck tape = duct tape

Straightjacket = straitjacket

These ones = these

Over-exaggerated = exaggerated

Cowtow = Kowtow

Slight of hand = sleight of hand

SCHOOL GRAFFITI

OEDIPUS WAS A NERVOUS REX.

Be alert - **your country needs lerts.**

Humpty Dumpty was pushed.

Humpty Dumpty sat on a wall
Humpty Dumpty had a great Fall
All the King's horses and all the King's men
Had scrambled eggs for the next four weeks

T.S. Eliot is an anagram of toilets

QUASIMODO – THAT NAME RINGS A BELL.

I wandered lonely as a cloud
because I had B.O.

Bo Peep did it for the insurance.

Mickey Mouse is a rat.

George Davis is ~~innos~~
~~inoss~~
guilty

Bad spellers of the world, untie

I used to use cliches all the time but now I avoid
them like the plague

Dyslexia lures, KO

**Roget's Thesaurus dominates, regulates, rules, OK,
all right, adequately**

THE JOYS OF ENGLISH COMPOSITION

Tarzan is a short name for the American flag – the full name is
Tarzan Stripes.

Both his legs were cut off and both his hands, most of his brains
were hanging through the side of his head and he was lying on
his bed – crying.

My aunt has been unduly disturbed of late, having two small children through the utter carelessness of the local dustmen.

A criminal is someone who gets caught.

He was a man of about 35 years of age, looked twenty and was forty.

As he walked quietly through the room, he heard the sound of heavy breeding.

It was a wonderful sensation sitting on such a high-powered bike with the power of 1,000 cubic centimetres throbbing between my legs.

The army captain was always putting his privates through such terrible exercises.

Some of the girls wear very short miniskirts but underneath they are the same as the next woman.

My mother said I could avenue coat for Christmas.

We had a longer holiday than usual this year because the school was closed for altercations.

We sat down to a picnic dinner of fricken chicasee.

I glanced at the grandfather clock in my waistcoat pocket.

They gave him enough money to have a strong drink and relieve himself.

I was nervous but eventually gathered up my guts and spoke to him.

A wife should be understanding, loving and bare with her husband.

When the amplifiers are turned up at full-blast, then everyone in the room evacuates.

People were running all over the place, the boys in shorts and the girls in hysterics.

After rowing across the bay, I slumped over the whores in a state of physical exhaustion.

As she went through her wardrobe, she found a scorpion in her drawers. She rose quickly.

I am not prepared to sit down and be made a convenience of.

When there are no fresh vegetables, you can always get canned.

It is bad manners to break your bread and roll in your soup.

At the age of seventeen I have finally been accepted by my family.

I used to use the sea as my convenience.

When my Mum was cutting the onions it made her ice water.

They were real diamonds which were worth their weight in gold.

This is a story of passion, bloodshed, desire, everything, in fact, that makes life worth living.

She was one of the finest women that ever walked the streets.

Newspapers also report calamities such as deaths, marriages etc.

It was the final straw in the camel's pack.

The Gorgons were three sisters who had long snakes for hair, tusks for teeth and claws for nails. They looked like women only more horrible.

I enjoyed my bondage with the family and especially with their mule, Jake.

The worst experience that I have probably ever had to go through emotionally was when other members of PETA (People for the Ethical Treatment of Animals) and I went to Pennsylvania for their annual pigeon shooting.

He was a modest man with an unbelievable ego.

Do you have trouble making up your mind? Well, yes and no.

My Mum has written to the Council to ask their permission to remove her drawers in the kitchen.

Such things as divorces, separations and annulments greatly reduce the need for adultery to be committed.

It is rewarding to hear when some of these prisoners I have fought for are released, yet triumphant when others are executed.

Playing the saxophone lets me develop technique and skill which will help me in the future since I would like to become a doctor.

However, many students would not be able to emerge from the same situation unscrewed.

'Bare your cross' – something I have heard all my life.

For almost all involved in these stories, premature burial had a negative effect on their lives.

Teaching at your school in your wonderfully gothic setting would be an exciting challenge.

My uncle has a catholic converter on his car.

Firemen started to fight the blaze with breathing apparatus.

My mother worked hard to provide me with whatever I needed in my life: a good home, a fairly stale family life and a wonderful education.

Must I shake the hand that has always bitten me?

In the spring, people were literally exploding inside.

The walls of the cathedral were supported by flying buttocks.

Stig informed the flight attendant that he wanted to sit near the isle.

Clapton extinguished himself on many early recordings.

Morse code was used in telepathy.

Celebrities can buy their own tropical islands but the rest of us hard-working morsels have to escape to a crowded beach.

The Church was destroyed by fire and the burning question was where the money would be found to rebuild it.

I felt my hair being yanked cruelly as I tumbled to the ground. Audrey's hate-crazed face hoovered over me.

The house was near to a main bus route, a short walk from the shops, had a garden, three bedrooms and two spacious deception rooms.

He looked almost square, as if his tailor had put too much pudding in the shoulders.

The speaker told of his adventure with a perilous bra constrictor.

The lady offered the seat on the bus and said she did not want to deprive the pupil of his seat. He assured her that there was no depravity.

My Mother bought all our clothes from the 'Army & Navy Surplus Store' – good quality but it was embarrassing going to school dressed as a Japanese General.

The Merchant of Venice was a famous Italian who bought and sold canal boats.

I never went through that terrible phase most girls experience. I went from child to woman in one go. One day I was a child, the next a man. *(Woman and Home)*

Although written many years ago, *Lady Chatterley's Lover* has just been re-issued by Grove Press, and this fictional account of the day-by-day life of an English gamekeeper is still of considerable interest to outdoor-minded readers, as it contains many passages on pheasant raising, the apprehending of poachers, ways to control vermin, and other chores and duties of the professional gamekeeper. Unfortunately, one is obliged to wade through many pages of extraneous material in order to discover and savour these highlights on the management of a Midland shooting estate, and in this reviewer's opinion, the book cannot take the place of J.R. Miller's *Practical Gamekeeper*. *(Review in the American magazine Field and Stream)*

ABOUT BOOKS

'Tell me, why did you become a printer?' 'I just seemed the right type.'

Shelley – *Prometheus Unbound* 6.99. Bound £11.99

> *Holy Scripture, Writ Divine*
> *Leather bound at two pounds nine.*
> *Satan trembles when he sees*
> *Bibles sold as cheap as these.*

Asking a working writer what he thinks about critics is like asking a lamp-post what it feels about dogs. *(John Osborne)*

His books are selling like wildfire. Everybody's burning them.

He was a man whose works were so little known as to be almost confidential.

A 'classic' is a book which people praise but don't read. *(Mark Twain)*

He said the printer had 'read off the wrong line', but promised that arrangements were already in hadna ot hvae tch netx edition printed korrectly. (Saturday *Telegraph*)

When my husband reads in bed on warm nights he puts a colander over his head. He says it keeps off the flies, shades his eyes from the light and lets in air at the same time. *(Letter in Good Shopping)*

Abraham Lincoln used to express gratitude to authors who sent him copies of their books and, after thanking each cordially, added: 'Be sure that I shall lose no time in reading it.'

I don't think anyone should write his autobiography until after he's dead. *(Sam Goldwyn)*

If a book about 'Failures' doesn't sell, then is it a success?

Don't judge a book by its movie.

Never lend books, for no one ever returns them; the only books I have in my library are books other folk have lent me. (*Anatole France*)

Some recent odd and unusual book titles:

Spit in the Ocean by Saul Singer

The Man Who Ate the 747 by Ben Sherwood

Eat That Frog by Brian Tracy

Do Plastic Surgeons Take Visa? by Kathy Peel

Warping, All By Myself by Cay Garrett

Matter of the Colon by Debora L. Meehan

Basic TIG and MIG Welding by Ivan Griffin

P.I.G. (Petrified Intestinal Gas) by Jurgen Grasshoff

Wrinkle-Faced Bats by Julie Murray

Atlas of the Lunar Terminator by John E. Westfell

I was a Teenage Fairy by Francesca Lia Block

Uncle Bob Talks with My Digestive System by Bob Devine and Barbara Cunningham

Ice Around Our Lips: Finland-Swedish Poetry by David McDuff

How I Cured Deadly Toe Nail Fungus by Mike Teeton

How To Lose Friends and Alienate People by Toby Young

And a final story about books:

A girl went into a library, approached the reception desk and demanded: 'A burger and chips, please.' The librarian looked at her and said, 'Do you realise this is a library?' The girl seemed to realise her mistake and whispered very quietly: 'A burger and chips, please.'

ABBREVIATIONS AND TRANSLATIONS

Su Doku mania exploded in France in July 2005 when it was published in Le Figaro, which explained that the 'nouvel jeu cerebral' had arrived by way of the English Channel. However, one drawback for the publishers was the name. Pronounced in French, the game sounds like 'suc du cul', which translates politely as 'sweats from the bum'. Here are some attempts by English children to interpret commonly heard phrases and abbreviations.

Infra dig – In lodgings

Pax in bello – freedom from stomach ache

Joie de vivre – whisky

B.Sc. – Boy Scout; Bachelor's Scholarship

PS – Piccadilly Circus; police station; please stop

Festina lente – The festival of Lent

Coup de grâce– A lawn mower

Sub judice – the bench on which the judges sit

B.A. – back ache; before Adam

K.G. – King of Greece

Etc. – a sign used when a person pretends to know more than they really do

C.O.D. – Collector of Debts

Raison d'être – The right to live

Les oiseaux chantaient dans les arbres – The oysters were singing in the trees

Pas de deux – Father of twins

Mal de mer – A bug caught from your mother

Fait accompli – Completed garden party

Esprit de corps – embalming fluid

Crudités – genitals

Fin de siècle – tail-light of a bicycle

Apéritif – dentures

Beau Geste – big joke

Bien – French vegetable

Carte blanche – white wheelbarrow

Chateau – French conversation

Fruits de mer – seaweed

Grand prix – large reward

À la carte – served from the trolley

Marseillaise – a French salad dressing

Pâté de foie gras – an outdoor circus held in New Orleans

Son et lumiere – your son is alight

Table d'hôte – hot plate

Mata Hari – means suicide in Japanese

Sotto voce – in a drunken voice

Terracotta – fear of beds

Par excellence – very good father

Achtung – my mouth hurts

But perhaps we should give the last word, for now, to Miles Kington.

Bonjour. Parlez –vous Franglais? C'est un doddle. Si vous etes un fluent English speaker, et si vous avaez un 'O'Level francais, Franglais est un morceau de gateau. Un 'O'Level de French est normalement inutile. Un nothing. Un wash-out. Les habitants de la France ne parlent pas 'O' Level French. Ils ne comprennent pas 'O' level French. Un 'O'Level en francais est un passeport a nowhere.

ALTERNATIVE DEFINITIONS

Accomplish – a fellow alcoholic.

Adorn – what comes after the darkest hour.

Age – something which disproves the theory that what goes up must come down.

Archaeologist – someone whose career's in ruins.

Baldness – hair today, gone tomorrow.

Bigamist – someone who has lived two well.

Cannibal – someone who is fed up with people.

Cockerel – an alarm cluck.

Conductor – a man who always faces the music.

Dead Ringer – an unwelcome Avon lady.

Debate – something to lure de fish.

Denial – Egypt's main river.

Designer stubble – an excuse for being too lazy to shave.

Eskimo – one of God's frozen people.

Fjord – a car made in Europe.

Forger – someone who writes wrongs.

Germicide – a virus that kills itself.

Giraffe – an animal head and shoulders above the others.

Grammar – your mother or father's Mam.

Granary – home for old ladies.

Gravely ill – someone suffering from mourning sickness.

Guillotine – a French chopping centre.

Hair salon – a place where women go to curl up and dye.

Highland fling – tossing the caber.

Himalaya – a very confused Italian cockerel.

Hippodrome – where to catch flying hippopotami.

Hollow – an empty greeting.

Hypochondria – someone who is allergic to good health.

Indentures – fashionable false teeth.

Insanity – a hereditary disease you get from your children.

Jumper – what you are told to put on when your mother feels cold.

Kayak – something an Eskimo can't have and eat at the same time.

Kindred – inborn fear of family relatives.

Knuckle down – feathers that grow on the back of the hand.

Kumquat – inevitable, as in kumquat may.

Leading question – shall we dance . . .?

Liable – the capacity to tell untruths.

Lynching – trial by fury.

Mammary – Rest home for tired Mams.

Man overboard – a mere drip in the ocean.

Melancholy – a sad sheepdog.

Mews – catty remarks.

Microwave – an almost imperceptible movement of the hand.

Minnehaha – a quick laugh.

Miser – Someone who lives in poverty so that he can die rich.

Moose – a Scottish rodent.

Naked truth – the bare facts.

Narrow-minded – having tunnel vision.

Pedestrian – a motorist who has found somewhere to park.

Poached egg – a thief's breakfast.

Polyphony – a budgie that thinks it's a parrot.

Quadruplets – four crying out loud.

Rear Admiral – a back-seat naval officer.

Rebore – to tell the same story over and over again.

Rock festival – a convention of geologists.

Shamrock – an imitation diamond.

Slippery – a shoe cupboard.

Soviet – a Russian napkin.

Stay of execution – to keep one's head when all about are losing theirs.

Toboggan – the reason for attending an auction.

Turncoat – a reversible jacket.

Twit – part of an owl's call.

Uncharted – a record which fails to get into the top 50.

Unsuited – naked.

Wheeler-dealer – second-hand car salesman.

Wolf whistle – a piercing noise made by wild dogs.

Yankee Doodle – an American cartoon.

Yucca – an expression of disgust.

3

Other Subjects

GEOGRAPHY

People who live on the Equator are called Equestrians.

The inhabitants of Moscow are called Mosquitoes.

The people of Israel are Israelites, the people of Canaan are Canaanites, and the people of Paris are called Parasites

Certain areas of the desert are cultivated by irritation.

The general direction of the Alps is straight up.

Most of the houses in France are made of plaster of Paris.

Persian cats are the chief industry of Persia, hence the word 'purr'.

In Holland the people make use of water power to drive their windmills.

There are three kinds of Downs – North Downs, South Downs and Eider Downs.

A virgin forest is a place where the hand of man has never set foot.

The climate of the islands is wet but embracing.

Crewe is the biggest conjunction in England.

The Sewage Canal is in Egypt.

The horizon is a line where the earth and the sky meet, but disappear when you get there.

The Specific Ocean borders the west coast of the United States.

China has so many Chinese that forced birth patrol is required.

The Temperate Zone is the region where no one drinks too much.

Britain has a temporary climate.

The three highest mountains in Scotland are Ben Nevis, Ben Lomond and Ben Jonson.

A blizzard is when it snows sideways.

Name three of the English lakes: Ullswater, Derwent Water and Bayswater.

A fissure is a man who sells fish.

In Egypt, one of the chief damned places is Aswan.

England has always been a nation of shoplifters.

The chief bays in the South of England are Torbay, Poole Bay and Bombay.

The Pyramids are a range of mountains between France and Spain.

Reefs are what you put on the top of coffins.

Geneva was a beautiful lady from Coventry who sometimes rode a white horse.

Mushrooms always grow in damp places and so they look like umbrellas.

In the middle of the 18th century, all the morons moved to Utah.

The Indians live very froogley.

A welsher is a person from Wales.

Mt Elgon National Park is well known for its rich deposits of herds of elephant.

GEOGRAPHY PLUS

Sarajevo isn't Hawaii. *(Bobby Robson)*

Playing with wingers is more effective against European sides like Brazil than sides like Wales. (*Ron Greenwood*)

According to legend, Telford is so dull that the bypass was built before the town. *(Victor Lewis-Smith)*

Best man was the bridegroom's brother, Mr Martin Gasson. The reception was at Langford's Hotel, Hove and the couple are honeymooning in Grease. *(Shoreham Herald)*

Due to a tree on the line, delays are occurring on the Wimbledon branch. *(Radio announcement)*

Brighton – a town that looks like it's helping police with their enquiries. *(Keith Waterhouse)*

I passed through Glasgow on the way here and couldn't help noticing how different it was from Venice. *(Raymond Asquith)*

Radio host: So, Becky where are you from?
Caller: Uganda.
Radio host: Oh, I thought you were from Africa.

Morecambe – a cemetery with lights. *(Anon)*

Brighton – God's Waiting Room. *(Anon)*

If I owned Texas and Hell, I would rent out Texas and live in Hell. *(General Philip H. Sheridan)*

In Australia, not reading poetry is the national pastime. *(P. McGinley)*

An English traveller inquired peevishly of a native on a very wet day in Scotland if it always rained in that country. 'No,' replied the Highlander, 'it *snows* sometimes.'

There are still parts of Wales where the only concession to gaiety is a striped shroud. *(Gwyn Thomas)*

We have flower battles just as they do in Nice. Only here we throw the pots as well. *(Brendan Behan, on the Dublin Festival)*

There's nothing Vichy about the French. *(Ivor Novello)*

Iraq: Things are going from Iraq to ruin *(Anon.)*

Holland . . . lies so low they are only saved by being damned *(Thomas Hood)*

On a clear day, from the terrace . . .you can't see Luxembourg at all. This is because a tree is in the way. *(Alan Coren)*

GEOGRAPHICAL GRAFFITI

Harwich for the Continent!
Dover for the incontinent!

Save Trees – Eat a Beaver

**WHAT YOU SHOULD DO
IF THE THAMES FLOODS**
– breast stroke

It's quicker by snail
(On British Rail poster)

HISTORY

Alexander the Great was born in the absence of his parents.

By a trick the Persians were enjuiced to attack.

The principal thing which was left behind by the Egyptians were their bones.

The Greeks had myths – myths are female moths.

Actually, Homer was not written by Homer but by another man of that name.

Athens had a democracy. This meant the citizens took the law into their own hands.

Julius Caesar was renowned for his great strength. He threw a bridge over the Rhine.

People called them Romans because they did not stay in one place for very long.

Latin is the language of the dead.

Hannibal is a well-known music writer.

Q: Where are the descendants of the ancient Britons to be found today?
A: In the British Museum.

Boudicea was a brave woman who fought herself and drove a chariot.

William the Conqueror was thrown from his horse and wounded in the feudal system and died of it.

William the Conqueror landed in 1066 A.D. and A.D. means after dark.

William I was the first Mormon King of England.

The Feudal System lies between the Humber and the Thames.

Prisons in the Norman period were not like ours; they were dull and dreary.

The Scotch hatted the English.

Prince Henry was drowned in the Wash. The story goes that he never smiled again.

At the coronation of Henry III, when the little King had been crowned, all his barons stood round and swore at him.

This happened I believe during the Industrial Resolution.

The victims of the Black Death grew boobs on their neck.

Florence Nightingale was a famous Swedish soprano.

Q: Where was Magna Carta signed?
A: At the bottom.

Bruce was a brave General and fought like a spider.

Joan of Arc was canonised by Bernard Shaw.

Joan the Arc was the daughter of a pheasant.

Joan of Arc was famous as Noah's wife.

Richard II was murdered in Pontefract Castle, but his fate is unknown.

It was Donatello's interest in the female nude which made him the father of the Renaissance.

Q: What do you know of Henry VIII?
A: I can't answer that question because we haven't done the Old Testament yet.

Now Henry had an abbess on his knee, which made walking difficult.

Henry, with the help of Thomas Cromwell, set about dissolusioning the monasteries.

Being a lady-in-mating gave a young girl a better chance of marriage.

My favourite character in English history is Henry VIII because he had eight wives and killed them all.

Henry VIII was a broad-shouldered man. Mary Tudor was a narrow-minded woman.

Henry VIII's third wife was Anne of Cleavage.

Henry said: 'Beware of the Brides of March'.

Sir Thomas More was a Roman Catholic executed by Henry VIII. He has now been carbonised by the Pope.

Q: Where are the Kings of England crowned?
A: On their heads.

Queen Elizabeth I exposed herself before her soldiers at Tilbury. They all shouted 'hurrah'.

Queen Elizabeth I never married. She had a very peaceful reign.

After Sir Walter Raleigh had spread his cloak on the ground, Queen Elizabeth I remarked: 'I am afraid I have spoiled your cloak.' Sir Walter replied: 'Dieu et mon droit,' which means 'My God and you're right.'

Queen Elizabeth I was so fond of dresses she was never seen without one.

'The Golden Hind' and 'The Golden Fleece' are the names of English pubs.

The King was crowned in the Crystal Palace. He had a sepulchre in his hand.

Queen Mary had all the Protestants put under the steak.

The Invisible Armada was so called because you couldn't see it.

King James I was very unclean in his habits. He never washed his hands and married Anne of Denmark.

Guy's hospital was built to commemorate the Gunpowder Plot.

The King was not to order taxis without the consent of Parliament.

In the Great Fire of London, the worst flaming place was St Paul's Cathedral.

The Great Fire of London really did a lot of good because it purified the city of the dregs of the plague and burned down eighty-nine churches.

Lord Bacon was impeached for receiving brides.

The great Duke of Marlborough was a man of very fine character omitting his vices which were many.

During the French Revolution Marie Anne Twinette was beheaded.

It happened during the French Resolution.

During the Napoleonic Wars, crowned heads were trembling in their shoes.

Melba – where Napoleon was imprisoned.

In the 19th century people stopped reproducing by hand and started reproducing by machines.

Lincoln's mother died in infancy.

The Poll Tax was to be paid by everybody who had a head.

Clive committed suicide three times and after the third time they sent him to India.

The inflammability of the Pope was proclaimed by the Vatican.

Marshal Goering was a fat man because he was one of Hitler's stoutest supporters.

At the Treaty of Versailles, the German army was restricted to 6,600,000,000 men. This seems a lot but Germany was a big country.

Queen Victoria's reclining years were exemplary.

The sun never set on the British Empire because it is in the East and the sun sets in the West.

Q: Who was the first woman to fly solo across the Atlantic?
A: Mae West.

It's a hysterical fact that Hitler committed suicide in a Berlin Bunker.

Hitler shot himself in the bonker.

The war was all over bar the shooting.

Q: Who would reign if the King died?
A: The Queen, and if there was no Queen, then the Knave.

You have to keep a watch on the Swiss.

The French national anthem is the mayonnaise.

Chequers is a public house near Wales.

Guerrilla warfare means up to their monkey tricks.

The Navy is sometimes called the Senile Service.

Parliament is a place where men sit and disgust bills.

Universal suffrage means even the illegible have the vote.

The chief duties of an M.P. are to go to sleep when another man is speaking and to force his party into power.

The Pry Minister lives in Downing Street.

St Andrew is the patent saint of Scotland.

Q: What were the races which have dominated England since the Romans?
A: Epsom, Newmarket and Doncaster.

HISTORY PLUS

After a tour of treasures, the Dowager, Countess of Rosebery relaxed in a seventeenth century chair that once belonged to a Venetian Dog. *(Arab World)*

I asked recently what Anne Boleyn had two more of than Gladstone. The answer was 'fingers' because she had six fingers on one hand and Gladstone had one blown off in a shooting accident. Now I am asked by Mr F.H. Bennett of West Wimbledon what else Anne Boleyn had two more of than Gladstone. The answer is . . . the letter N. Well done Mr Bennett – and thank you very much. *(Daily Mail)*

An archaeologist is the best husband a woman can have; the older she gets, the more interested he is in her. *(Agatha Christie)*

One third of the houses have no fixed baths, or piped hot or cold water. And many have sanitation unchanged since Queen Victoria sat on the throne. *(Labour Woman)*

In my opinion he will make a great King. He is a young man wise beyond his ears. *(Armand Hammer on Prince Charles in the Sunday Times)*

The relationship between the Welsh and the English is based on trust and understanding. They don't trust us and we don't understand them. *(Dudley Wood)*

When Kruschev was in control in Russia he was condemning the evils of the reign of Stalin before a large audience. A voice called out, 'You were one of his colleagues. Why didn't you stop him?' A terrible silence followed during which no man moved a muscle.

Raking the audience with his eyes, Kruschev thundered, 'Who said that?' The tension became unbearable as not a man moved or spoke. Then Kruschev quietly said, 'Now you know why.'

Another story concerning Kruschev relates to a meeting of the United Nations in the 1960s. Harold Macmillan, speaking on behalf of the United Kingdom, was interrupted by Mr Kruschev, who, in order to emphasise his disagreement, hammered on his desk with the heel of one of his shoes. Calmly Macmillan asked the interpreters, 'I wonder whether I might have that translated?'

At the height of the Industrial Revolution (in the nineteenth century), child labour was prevalent in England's factories and coal mines. One day the famed industrialist and philanthropist Robert Owen encountered a twelve-year-old breaker boy, exhausted from separating shale from coal, completely covered in black coal dust. 'Do you know God?' Owen asked.

'No,' the boy replied respectfully. 'He must work in some other mine.'

I'm a centurion, toothbrush on the head. *(Eddie Izzard)*

How butch is an army that has a wine opener on its knife? *(Robin Williams on the Swiss Army)*

HISTORICAL GRAFFITI

**It's a good job that
William Ewart Gladstone is dead.
He's been buried an
awful long time**

**Why don't you give Elgin
his marbles back?**
(British Museum)

**Where is Lee Harvey Oswald
now that his country needs him?**
(During Iraq War)

Start a new movement – eat a prune

**In 1066, near this church, the Normans
landed and were repelled by the men of Romney
– so am I – Candice**

Just gone for a walk round the block – Anne Boleyn

THE GRAVE OF KARL MARX IS JUST ANOTHER COMMUNIST PLOT.

Beneath an advertisement on the London Underground showing Henry VIII buying a ticket and saying, 'Tower Hill return, please,' someone had added, *'And a single for the wife.'*

ROMANS GO HOME
(Hadrian's Wall)

MUSIC

There are the great composers like Bach, Handel and Mantovani.

Agnus Dei was a woman composer famous for her church music.

Refrain means don't do it – in music you better not try and sing.

Henry Purcell is a well-known composer few people have ever heard of.

Music sung by two people at the same time is called a duel.

I do know what a sextet is but I would rather not say.

My favourite composer is Opus.

An oboe is an American tramp.

A trumpet is a musical instrument when it is not an elephant noise.

Q: What are kettle drums called?
A: Kettle drums.

A bassoon looks like nothing I have ever heard.

I can't reach the brakes on this piano.

The correct way to find the key to a piece of music is to use a pitchfork.

A virtuoso is a musician with real high morals.

The most dangerous part of playing the cymbals is near the nose.

Just about any animal skin can be stretched over a frame to make a pleasant sound once the animal is removed.

MUSIC PLUS

Music was provided by the pipe band of Queen Victoria and the brass band of the First Battalion Gordon Highlanders. There was a complete absence of wind.

The school concert was a great success ... Special thanks are due to the Head's daughter who laboured the whole evening at the piano, which as usual fell upon her.

John Totten and his banjo, along with several friends and their banjos, will provide an instrumental interlude at St Bega's, which itself should be worth the price of admission (which, by the way, is free).

On the programme was the Limerick String Quartet with, as usual, their six members.

In the packed school hall parents stood listening to the orchestra when one barged into the back of the other. 'Who do you think you're pushing?' 'I don't know,' replied the jostler, 'What is your name?'

> *There was a young girl in the choir,*
> *Whose voice rose higher and higher,*
> *Till one Sunday night*
> *It rose out of sight,*
> *And they found it next day on the spire.*

Wagner's music is better than it sounds. *(Bill Nye)*

Signor Ravelli's first selection will be 'Somewhere My Love Lies Sleeping' with a male chorus.

I told him to leave my organ alone but he kept playing with the knobs.

One day when he was seven years old, the prodigious Mischa Elman was asked to give a violin recital for some family friends. He selected Beethoven's *Kreutser* sonata, which he played with ease and considerable virtuosity. During one of the piece's many pauses, one of his listeners, a kindly old woman, tapped Elman on the shoulder. 'Dear,' she whispered confidentially, 'play something you know.'

A true gentleman is a man who knows how to play the bagpipes – but doesn't.

While visiting a farm with his parents one day, Mozart heard a pig squeal. 'G-sharp!' he exclaimed. The curious party promptly ran to a piano; G-sharp it was. The budding composer was just two years old.

When Mozart was my age, he had already been dead for a year. *(Tom Lehrer)*

Bobby Robson, one-time England football manager, once tried to express his admiration of musicians: 'I would have given my right arm to be a pianist,' he said.

Dear Patron or Non-playing Member, the orchestra will be holding its annual cheese and wind party on Friday, June 16th at 8 p.m. *(Wilmslow & District Orchestral Society)*

Jubilee Brass Public Concert – at the Deaf Centre, St Ebbes, Wednesday March 1st at 7 p.m.

William Mann picks the early Shostakovich opera, *The Nose*, with a virtuoso performance by Eduard Akhimov. Robert Layton was also tempted to pick *The Nose*, but faced with so many Shostakovich novelties, settled for his song cycles. *(Soviet Weekly)*

Infirmary Operatic Society – MALE MEMBERS – Urgently Required. *(Leicester Mercury)*

SHOWBOAT
Early March at Luton College
of Technology
WANTED
Actors, Singers, Dancers – Men Particularly
Stage Staff.
Sex immaterial but an advantage.
(The Luton Times)

MASSIVE ORGAN DRAWS CROWD *(Headline in Kent Messenger)*

Small Organs Trendy *(The Times)*

Madam, you have between your legs an instrument capable of giving pleasure to thousands – and all you can do is scratch it *(Sir Thomas Beecham to a lady cellist)*

The BBC Chorus sang with considerable punch in the tutties even if they left something to be desired when individual sections were exposed. *(Daily Telegraph)*

Top of the bill: Glen Campbell – 'The Nine Stone Cowboy' *(Stoke Evening Sentinel)*

The Ford Foundation announced today that it will give $85 to some 50 leading American symphony orchestras. The Foundation's President, Henry Heald, said no strings were attached to the grant. *(Daily Telegraph)*

The baritone voice of Mr Sender was thoroughly adapted to the 'Song of the Vulgar Boatman'. *(Cleveland Press)*

Mrs Steelman was again the honorary conductor and as long as she holds the reins of the School's Choral Society there need be no fear of success. *(The Lincoln Gazette)*

Of all the noises known to man, opera is the most expensive. *(Moliere)*

Don't get annoyed if your neighbour plays his drums at two o'clock in the morning. Telephone him at 4 a.m. and tell him how much you enjoyed it.

Mr D. Harris, playing solo trumpet in the Bedford Band, was awarded the medal for the best trombone player in the section.' *(Sheffield Telegraph)*

MUSIC GRAFFITI

Down with early Byzantine music.
(Cambridge)

To do is to be – Rousseau
To be is to do – Sartre
Do-be-do-be-do – Sinatra

Handel's Organ Works
(Notice in music library)
– so does mine.

Rodgers and Hammerstein rule, OK lahoma

RELIGION

The seventh commandment is thou shalt not admit adultery.

St Paul cavorted to Christianity.

The Bishop preached Holy Acrimony which is another name for marriage.

Lot's wife was a pillar of salt by day and a ball of fire by night.

The greatest miracle in the bible is when Joshua told his son to stand still and he obeyed.

Noah's Ark came to rest on Mount Arafat.

Q: Why do so few Asians play top-flight football?
A: It is because of religious reasons – they have to take off their turbines.

Zacharias was burning insects when he saw an angel.

Esau sold his copyright for a mess of potash.

Jacob didn't eat much except when there was a famine in the land.

Abraham was chiefly noted for his bosom.

The Philistines are islands in the Pacific.

The locusts were the chief plague. They ate all the first-born.

Solomon had 300 wives and 700 cucumbers.

Jacob had a brother called Seesaw.

The Primate is the wife of the Prime Minister.

Abraham was a bellowing sheep. *(Bedouin sheik)*

St Alban was the first British Martha.

Samuel was commanded to kill everybody. This he did in a half-hearted fashion as he nailed the king to a tree.

Salome was a lady who took off her clothes and danced before Harrods.

Q: What did the Israelites do when they emerged from the Red Sea?
A: They dried themselves.

The Israelites made a golden calf because they didn't have enough gold to make a cow.

The Pope is chosen by the Cardinals who form the electrical college.

The Jews received manna in their dessert during the flight from Egypt.

Q: Explain the meaning of bishop, priest and deacon.
A: I have never seen a bishop so I don't know. A priest is a man in the Old Testament and a deacon is something you set fire to on top of a hill.

As a Catholic priest, one spends most of his time teaching, praying, giving sermons, and absorbing sins.

Sodom and Gomorrah are two famous volcanoes in Europe.

A synagogue is a place like a church where sinners go.

An idolater is a very lazy person.

Moses was single but certainly a father in the desert.

One of the Christian virtues is humidity.

Faith – that quality which enables us to believe what we know to be untrue.

The priest turned to the people and said: 'Thanks Peter God.'

Good King Wenceslaus looked stout on the feast of Steven.

Moses went up Mount Cyanide.

Blessed are the meek for they shall inhibit the earth.

If the three Wise men had been women, I think they would have arrived on time, helped deliver the baby, cleaned the stable and brought disposable nappies as gifts.

In the story of the Prodigal Son, the younger son got together everything he had and left for a distant country, where he used up all his money on a life of debauchery . . . and then he squandered the rest.

Samson slew the Philistines with the axe of the Apostles.

The first commandment was when Eve told Adam to eat the apple.

Jesus' mother Mary was different because of her Immaculate Contraption.

Jesus wrote the 'B' Attitudes.

Michaelangelo painted scenes from the Bible on the roof of the Sixteen Chapel.

RELIGION PLUS

Jimmy Carter's Southern Baptist roots frequently led reporters to question his stance on moral issues. 'How would you feel if you were told that your daughter was having an affair?' a reporter once asked. 'Shocked and overwhelmed,' Carter replied. 'She's only seven years old.'

Thought For The Day – The whle wrod is in a state of chassis – Sean O'Casey *(The Rising Nepal)*

The International Clairvoyant Society (Brussels branch) has had to cancel next week's meeting, due to unforeseen circumstances. *(The Bulletin)*

'Hell to pay' if vicars go on strike. *(Southend Echo)*

Archbishop Sin named Cardinal. *(Bulletin Today Manila)*

Dr James Pike, the former Anglican Bishop of California who died recently in Israel, talks to Oliver Hunkin about psychic phenomena. *(The Listener)*

CH . . . CH. What's missing? U.R. (You are!) *(Sign outside a church)*

MADRID – Catholic nuns of the Mission of Jesus, Mary and Joseph, with a television success behind them and Mother Superior Francisca at the guitar, are bidding here for fame and fortune in the pope charts. *(Evening Post)*

HOLIDAY BLESSING – The Pope, who is spending his summer holiday at Castel Gandolfo, south of Rome, yesterday blessed all those who cannot afford a holiday. *(The Sun)*

Sermon tonight: It will be gin at 8 p.m. (*St. Pat's, Dipton*)

HARROW SCHOOL CHAPEL – NOT TO BE TAKEN AWAY *(Notice outside the church at the public school)*

The people of Macedonia did not believe so St Paul got stoned.

It often happens that I wake at night and begin to think about a serious problem and decide I must tell the Pope about it. Then I wake up completely and remember that I am the Pope. *(Pope John XXIII)*

There will be a procession next Sunday along the cliff top, but if it rains in the afternoon the procession will take place in the morning. (*St John's church, Bexhill.*)

Apologies to the Seventh day Adventist Church, Chiswick. In our 'Church Notes' last week we stated that the church had observed a day of 'prayer and feasting'. This should have read a day of 'prayer and fasting'. *(Brentford & Chiswick Times)*

A mother was making pancakes for her two sons, Kevin and Ryan. The boys began to argue over who would get the first pancake. Their mother saw this as an opportunity for a moral lesson. 'If Jesus was here he would say, "Let my brother have the first pancake. I can wait."'
    Kevin turned to his brother and said, 'Ryan, you can be Jesus.'

One day early in his career, Billy Graham arrived in a small town to preach a sermon. Wanting to post a letter, he approached a young lad in the street and asked him where there was a post box. After the boy had directed him to the local post office, Graham thanked him and invited him to attend the sermon. 'If you come to the Baptist church this evening,' he said, 'you can hear me telling everyone how to get to heaven.'

'I think I'll give it a miss,' the youngster replied. 'You don't even know your way to the post office!'

One morning while attending Timbertops School in Australia, Prince Charles attended a service at the local parish church. As the royal visitor left his church, the rector apologized for the small turnout: 'Being bank holiday weekend,' he explained, 'most of the parishioners are away.'

'Not another bank holiday!' the prince exclaimed. 'What's this one in aid of?'

'Well,' the rector replied, rather embarrassed, 'over here we call it the Queen's birthday.'

> *No matter how much I probe and prod*
> *I cannot quite believe in God,*
> *But oh! I hope to God that he*
> *Unswervingly believes in me!*
> *(E. Y. Harburg)*

I hear Glenn Hoddle has found God. That must have been a hell of a pass. *(Jasper Carrott)*

A monastic hospital in Belgium displayed notices in French, German and English. The English notice read: 'The Brothers of the Misericorde harbour every kind of disease and have no respect for religion.'

'The dispensation had to come from the Pope. Now what we both hoped for is actually coming true. Both my wife-to-be and myself, were, and still are, true and active alcoholics and we will continue to be so.' *(Yorkshire Post)*

It is related that John Knox, the famous Scottish Presbyterian, who fulminated from the pulpit against Mary Queen of Scots, imposed the strictest discipline on his family. On one occasion, when his daughter was late for breakfast, he greeted her with the words, 'Child of the Devil.'

'Good morning, father,' she replied.

Priest: Which Bible story do you like best, my son?
Youngster: The one about the fellow who just loafs and fishes.

First clergyman: When I preach I have them glued to their seats.
Second clergyman: Now why didn't I think of that?

Q: Who was the funniest man in the bible?
A: Samson – he brought the house down.

Some speakers electrify their listeners, others only gas them.

A Jewish boy comes home and tells his mother he has got a part in the school play. 'Wonderful', says the mother, 'What part is it?'

The boy says, 'I play the part of the Jewish husband.'

The mother scowls and tells him, 'Go back and tell your teacher you want a speaking role.'

The nuns took the class of six-year-olds to the local church to have a look around. At one end they placed a bowl of apples and at the other a bowl of biscuits and invited the children to take one or the other. As William approached the apples, he was reminded by Sister Gertrude that he should take only one because 'Jesus was watching them'. He did so, then made straight for the biscuits, where he told his friend: 'Take as many of these as you want – He's keeping an eye on the apples.'

I do benefits for all religions –I'd hate to blow the hereafter on a technicality. *(Bob Hope)*

SOME CHURCH NOTICES

The Associate Minister unveiled the church's new tithing campaign slogan last Sunday: 'I Upped My Pledge – Now Up Yours'.

The Church is starting a New Young Mother's Group. Anyone desiring to be a New Young Mother is to meet with the Pastor in the office.

Allison Belch, a missionary from Africa, will be speaking tonight at the Calvary Memorial Church in Racine. Why not come and hear Allison Belch all the way from Africa?

There will be a National PRAYER & FASTING Conference: The cost for attending the conference includes meals.

Irving Benson and Jessie Carter were married on October 24 in the church. So ended a friendship that began in their school days.

Eight new choir robes are currently needed, due to the addition of several new members and the deterioration of some older ones.

The Lutheran men's group will meet at 6 p.m. Steak, mashed potatoes, green beans and dessert will be served for a nominal feel.

The ladies of the Church have 'cast off old clothing' of every kind. They may be seen in the basement on Friday afternoon.

This evening at 7 p.m. there will be a hymn-sing in the park opposite the Church. Bring a blanket and come prepared to sin.

For those who have children and don't know it, we have a nursery downstairs.

Weight Watchers will meet at 7 p.m. at the First Presbyterian Church. Please use large double door at the side entrance.

The altar boy asked the priest, 'Father, do you know how many people are dead in the cemetery?' Before the priest could give a considered response, the lad said, 'All of them.'

A tactless priest was comforting grieving relatives after the crematorium service. 'I'll pop around to see you once the dust has settled.'

SOME EPITAPHS

Sacred to the memory of
MAJOR JAMES BRUSH
who was killed by the
accidental discharge
of a pistol by
his orderly
14th of April 1831
Well done thou good and
Faithful servant

**She lived with her husband of fifty years
And died in the confident hope of a better life**

Alice Mary Johnson 1883–1947
Let her **RIP**

Here lies the body of
THOMAS VERNON
The only surviving son
Of
Admiral Vernon
Died 23rd of July, 1753

**GOOD KNIGHT
GOING
GOING
GONE
1868**
(On the tombstone of an auctioneer named Knight at Greenwood)

Erected to the memory of
JOHN PHILIPS
accidentally shot
as a mark of affection by
his brother

**Stranger, tread this ground with
Gravity,
Dentist Brown is filling his last
Cavity.**
(Tombstone in St George's Church, Edinburgh)

**Here lies an honest lawyer.
That is Strange.**
(Epitaph of barrister John Strange)

**Blown upward
Out of sight
He sought the leak
By candlelight**
(Cemetery in Collingbourne)

**Here I lie and no wonder I'm dead
For the wheel of the wagon ran over my head.**
(On grave in Prendergast, Wales)

**In loving memory of my beloved
Wife, Hester; the mother of Edward,
Richard, Mary, Penelope, John, Henry,
Michael, Susan, Emily, Charlotte,
Amelia, George, Hugh, Hester,
Christopher and Daniel. She was a
great breeder of pugs, a devoted
Mother and a dear friend.**
(Hemel Hempstead)

**He died in peace
His wife died first**
(Gravestone in Ilfracombe)

**In Loving Memory of Frank Stainer
Of Staffordshire
Who left us in peace Feb. 2nd, 1910**

**After a short, difficult and useless life,
Here rests in the Lord
Robert Tweddle. 1735, aged 32.**
(Haltwhistle, Northumberland)

Jonathan Grober.
Died dead sober.
Lord thy wonders never cease.

Here lies the body of Charlotte Greer,
Whose mouth would stretch from ear to ear.
Be careful as you tread this sod,
For if she gapes, you're gone, by God.

I am ready to meet my Maker. Whether my Maker is prepared for the ordeal of meeting me is another matter. *(Winston Churchill on his 75th birthday)*

Either this man is dead or my watch has stopped. *(Groucho Marx)*

Ernie: What would you like them to put on your tombstone?
Eric: Something short and simple.
Ernie: What?
Eric: Back in Five Minutes.

HOLY GRAFFITI

A man's best friend is his dogma

Be Baptised with the Holy Spirit
Why waste
good whisky?

Religion is the opium of the peoplezzzzzzzzzzzz

Work for the Lord – The pay is terrible
but the fringe benefits are out of this world!

**WHERE WILL YOU BE ON
THE DAY OF JUDGEMENT?**
Still here waiting for the No.10 bus!

**CHURCH OF ST EDWARD
Are you tired of sin
and longing for a rest?**
If not, Phone Bayswater 36423

**Don't blame God –
he's only human**

(Outside a Cardiff chapel had been erected a placard)

Drink is thine enemy.
(Someone added overnight)
Thou shalt love thine enemies.

**80% OF BISHOPS TAKE THE TIMES
– the other 20% buy it.**

**Prayer meeting at 7.30 on Wednesdays.
Refreshments provided afterwards
– come to pray, stay to scoff.**

The Rev. Charles Spurgeon Departed For Heaven at 6.30 a.m. Today.

10.45 a.m. Not yet arrived. Getting anxious, Peter

(Metropolitan Tabernacle, London)

Adam met Eve and turned over a new leaf.

(Broadstairs)

ESKIMOS ARE GOD'S FROZEN PEOPLE

(Greenwich)

The Meek Shall Inherit The Earth – but not the mineral rights

(Attributed to J. Paul Getty)

SOME CHILDREN'S LETTERS TO GOD

Dear God . . .

Did you really mean the giraffe to have such a long neck or was it an accident?

Please make it that dogs live as long as people.

Is it true my Dad won't go to heaven if he uses his football match words in the house?

Who draws the lines around countries?

I went to this wedding and they were kissing right on the altar – is that OK?

When you said 'do unto others as you would do unto yourself', did you really mean it? Because if you did then I am really going to fix my brother.

Thank you for the little baby brother but I really did want a puppy.

Dear Sir, Can you show me how paint comes off?

It rained for the whole of our holiday and my Dad said some pretty bad things about you that I think people are not supposed to say. I hope you will not hurt him anyway. Your friend (but I'm not going to tell you who I am).

Why is Sunday school on Sunday? I thought it was supposed to be our day of rest.

Please send me a pony. I never asked for anything before. You can look it up.

Remember when the snow was deep and we didn't have to go to school. Could we have it again?

If you give me a genie lamp like Aladdin, I will give you anything you want except my money or my chess set.

We read that Thomas Edison made the light. I thought you did.

Dear God, Count me in. Your friend, Herbie.

My brother is a rat – can you give him a tail? Ha, ha.

What are colds for?

I want to be just like you when I grow up. OK?

When I grow up I would like to be like my Dad – only can I have plenty of hair on my head?

My father can never get a fire started. Could you make a burning bush in our yard?

I think the stapler is one of your greatest inventions.

On Halloween I am going to wear a Devil's costume. Is that all right with you?

Do plastic flowers make you mad? *I* would be if I made the real ones.

If you watch me in church on Sunday, I'll show my new shoes.

I read your book. It is called the Bible.

I would like to live for 900 years like the guy in the bible.

I would like to be a teacher so I can boss people around.

Can you marry food?

How do you feel about people who don't believe in you? Somebody else wants to know.

I know that God loves everybody but he's never met my sister.

Mrs Coe got a new refrigerator. We got the box it came in for a club house. So that's where I'll be if you are looking for me.

If you don't take the baby back I won't clean my room.

Why isn't Mrs God in the bible? Weren't you married to her when you wrote it?

Christmas should be earlier because kids can only be good for so long.

My father should be a minister because each day he gives us a sermon.

Are there any devils on earth because I think there is one in my class?

I want to get married but no one will do it with me.

Instead of letting people die and having to make new ones, why don't you just keep the ones you've got now?

SCIENCES

Genetics explains why you look like your father and, if you don't, why you should.

Depth is height upside down.

Q: What are 'involuntary muscles'?
A: They are not as willing as voluntary ones.

When you breathe, you inspire. When you do not breathe then you expire.

The dodo is a bird which is almost decent by now.

Q: Give an example of a movement in plants?
A: Triffids

The spinal column is a long bunch of bones. The head sits on the top and you sit on your bottom.

A trapezium is what they swing on in a circus.

Dew is formed on leaves when the sun shines down on them and makes them perspire.

Iron was discovered because someone smelt it.

The universe is a giant orgasm.

H_2O is hot water, and CO_2 is cold water.

For dog bite: put the dog away for several days. If he has not recovered, then kill it.

Artificial insemination is when the farmer does it to the cow instead of the bull.

Sir Isaac Newton invented gravity.

Galileo dropped his balls to prove gravity.

The census is sight, taste, touch, smell and hearing.

To collect the fumes of sulphur hold a deacon over a flame in a test tube.

A circle is a line which meets its other end without ending.

Marie Curie did her research at the Sore Buns Institute in Paris.

The Earth makes one resolution every 24 hours.

When you smell an odourless gas it is probably carbon monoxide.

Algebraical symbols are used when you do not know what you are talking about.

A triangle which has an angle of 135 degrees is called an obscene triangle.

A magnet is something you find crawling all over a dead cat.

When people run around and around in circles we say they are crazy. When planets do it we say they are orbiting.

In some rocks you can find the fossil footprints of fishes.

One of the main causes of dust is janitors.

Q: How is eye colour etc. passed to the next generation?
A: By the jeans (not Levis).

Q: What liquid goes around the body?
A: Liquid nitrogen.

A super-saturated solution is one that holds more than it can hold.

The four seasons are salt, pepper, mustard and vinegar.

Parallel lines never meet unless you bend one or both of them.

Q: Is a brick a solid, a liquid or a gas?
A: Yes.

Blood consists of two kinds of corkscrews – red corkscrews and white corkscrews.

A circle is a round straight line with a hole in the middle.

To remove air from a flask, fill the flask with water, tip the water out and put the cork in quick.

Q: What happens when the human body is completely submerged in water?
A: The telephone rings.

Polygon – a man with several wives or a dead parrot.

Water is composed of two gins –Oxygin and Hydrogin. Oxygin is pure gin, Hydrogin is gin and water.

Hydrogen is colourless, odourless and insolvent.

The mechanical advantage of a long pump handle is that you can have someone to help you pump.

We are now masters of time and eccentricity.

Q: Explain the meaning of 'erg'.
A: When people are playing football and you want them to do their best, you 'erg' them on.

It is easy to stall a car if you open your throttle before you are engaged.

Heat is transmitted by conviction.

One horsepower is the amount of energy it takes to drag a horse 500 feet in one second.

For fainting: Rub the person's chest, or if a lady, rub her arm above the hand instead.

To remove dust from the eye: Pull the eyelid down over the nose.

I'm drawing a racoon – one of those things butterflies come out of.

The fertiliser spreader has a revolving bottom.

You can listen to thunder after lightning and tell how close you came to getting hit. If you don't hear it you got hit, so never mind.

Some people can tell what time it is by looking at the sun. But I have never been able to make out the numbers.

In looking at a drop of water under a microscope, we find there are twice as many H's as O's.

It is important not to sleep with any old person.

It is possible to dry angleworms until they are only 46 per cent water, and still revive them, but they die if they become one-fifth of 1 per cent drier than 46 per cent.

A vibration is a motion that can't make up its mind which way it wants to go.

SCIENCE GRAFFITI

Horse power rules, neigh neigh.

(Beverley race course)

Poor little Tommy Jones

We'll see him no more

For what he thought was H_2O

Was H_2SO_4

4

Sport

We're going to have to use our heads a bit more when we bat. *(Nasser Hussain)*

Well Clive, it's all about the two M's. Movement and positioning. *(Ron Atkinson)*

If Glenn Hoddle said anything to his team at half time, it was concentration and focus. *(Ron Atkinson)*

Michael Owen – he's got the legs of a salmon. *(Craig Brown)*

I've seen some players with very big feet, and some with very small feet. *(David Pleat)*

Pires has got something about him: he can go both ways depending on who's facing him. *(David Pleat)*

Goalkeepers aren't born today until they're in their late twenties or thirties and sometimes not even then. *(Kevin Keegan)*

Chile have three options – they could win or they could lose. *(Kevin Keegan)*

I came to Nantes two years ago and it's much the same today, except that it's completely different. *(Kevin Keegan)*

Zidane is not very happy, because he's suffering from the wind. *(Kevin Keegan)*

Despite his white boots, he has pace and aggression. *(Kevin Keegan)*

In life he was a living legend; in death, nothing has changed. *(Barry Venison)*

When you're 4–0 up you should never lose 7–1. *(Lawrie McMenemy)*

Arnie Palmer, usually a great putter, seems to be having trouble with his long putts. However, he has no trouble dropping his shorts. *(US golf commentator)*

Billy Jean has always been conscious of wind on the centre court. *(Dan Maskell)*

Maradona gets tremendous elevation with his balls, no matter what position he's in. *(David Pleat)*

What I said to them at half time would be unprintable on the radio. *(Gerry Francis)*

Girls shouldn't play with men's balls – their hands are too small. *(Senator Wally Horn on basketball)*

The problem with intersexual swimming is that the boys often outstrip the girls.

Running is a unique experience, and I thank God for exposing me to the track team.

Gascoigne has pissed a fartness test. *(Bob Wilson)*

They're two points behind us so we're neck and neck. *(Bobby Robson)*

Apart from their goals, Norway haven't scored. *(Terry Venables)*

I think this could be our best victory over Germany since the war. *(John Motson)*

Bruce has got the taste of Wembley in his nostrils. *(John Motson)*

So different from the scenes in 1872, at the Cup Final none of us can remember. *(John Motson)*

Actually, none of the players are wearing earrings. Kjeldberg, with his contact lenses, is the closest we can get.' *(John Motson)*

As the four finalists hit the bend in the 1500 metres race, Thomson produced an electrifying bust which swept him past his opponents into the home straight to breast the tape. *(Camarthen Journal)*

Ampleforth elected to bath first on a pitch damp on top from the early rain. *(Wolverhampton Express and Star)*

I love sports. Whenever I can, I watch the Detroit Tigers on the radio. *(Gerald Ford)*

Sports Focus apologises for getting its wires crossed last week, and would like to make the following correction to the quote of the week: 'Saddam Hussain is not the England cricket captain – He is the leader of Iraq.' We meant to say 'Nasser Hussein'.

FRONT PAGE SPORT

So who ever broke a leg at golf? ALAN SMITH EVERY SUN-DAY *(The People)*

INJURY FORCES MISS TRUMAN TO SCRATCH *(Hartlepool Mail)*

MARY'S TWO BOOBS SINK BRITAIN *(The Sun)*

This does not detract from the achievements of the charging Eton bowler, whose balls came off the pitches so fast batsmen were hustled into errors. *(Marlborough Review)*

The most one-footed player since Long John Silver. *(Comment on Savo Milosevic in Birmingham Evening Mail)*

You are talking about a man who spelled his name wrong on his transfer request. *(West Brom manager Gary Megson on player Jason Roberts)*

As a small boy I was torn between two ambitions; to be a footballer or to run away and join a circus. At Partick Thistle I got to do both. *(Alan Hansen)*

Yurrrgggggh! *Der stod Ingelland!* Lord Nelson! Lord Beaverbrook! Winston Churchill! Henry Cooper! Clement Attlee! Anthony Eden! Lady Diana! *Der stod dem all! Der stod dem all!* Maggie Thatcher, can you hear me? Can you hear me, Maggie? Your boys took one hell of a beating tonight. *(Borg Lillelien, Norwegian commentator, Norway 2, England 1, 1981)*

ACLCOHOLISM V COMMUNISM *(Banner waved by Scotland fans versus the USSR, 1982)*

You could put his knowledge of the game on a postage stamp. He wanted us to sign Salford Van Hire because he thought he was a Dutch international. *(Fred Ayre on unnamed Wigan Athletic football director)*

Personally, I have always looked on cricket as organised loafing. *(Future Archbishop of Canterbury William Temple when he was Headmaster of Repton, c.1914)*

Cricket is the only game you can put on weight while playing. *(Tommy Docherty)*

It's a funny kind of month, October. For the keen cricket fan it's when you realise your wife left you in May. *(Denis Norden)*

Grandmother or tails, sir? *(Anonymous rugby referee to Princess Anne's son Peter Phillips, Gordonstoun School's rugby captain, at pre-match coin toss)*

Chairman of the Bored *(Comment by The Herald Sun, Sydney, on Clive Woodward)*

James Dudgeon of Lincoln City was sent off for a booable offence. *(Grimsby Sports Telegraph)*

I would like to thank the press from the heart of my bottom. *(Nick Faldo after winning the Open in 1992)*

Ernie: You know what your main trouble is?
Eric: What?
Ernie: You stand too close to the ball after you've hit it.

Tiger Woods won his first international tournament at the age of eight. This was not his first tournament victory, however. That came in a ten-and-under tournament – when Tiger was two years old.

And now over to ringside, where Harry Commentator is your carpenter. *(Unknown BBC link-up man)*

Sure there have been injuries and deaths in boxing, but none of them serious. *(Alan Minter)*

Tommy Cooper: I was in the ring once with Cassius Clay, and I got him worried.
Henry Cooper: Oh, really?
Tommy Cooper: He thought he'd killed me.

If you want to see what you'll look like in another ten years, look in the mirror after you've run a marathon. *(Jeff Scaff)*

And the line-up for the final of the women's 400 metres hurdles includes three Russians, two East Germans, a Pole, a Swede and a Frenchman. *(David Coleman)*

Zola Budd: so small, so waif-like, you literally can't see her. But there she is. *(Alan Parry)*

I was watching Sumo wrestling on the television for two hours before I realised it was darts. *(Hattie Hayridge, comedienne)*

This is really a lovely horse. I once rode her mother. *(Ted Walsh, commentator)*

My word, look at that magnificent erection! *(Brough Scott on the new stand at the Doncaster course)*

Willie Carson, riding his 180th winner of the season, spent the last two furlongs looking over one shoulder then another, even between his legs, but there was nothing there to worry him. *(Sporting Life)*

I backed a horse today at five to one – it came in at ten past four. *(Tommy Cooper)*

And the victorious crew celebrate in the traditional manner – dipping their cox into the Thames. *(The Guardian)*

I am getting to the age when I can only enjoy the last sport left. It is called 'hunting for your spectacles'. *(Sir Edward Grey)*

And finally . . .

A local junior football coach in the northeast of England used the same opening speech every year: 'We have to act as sportsmen at all times. There will be no yelling at the referees or other players and no being poor losers. Is that understood?' At that point the kids would nod, then the coach would add, 'Good. Now, please go home and explain all that to your parents.'

5

Careers

WANTED – Some additional female technicians at the fast-expanding Charles River Breeding Laboratory. No previous experience necessary. *(Advert in Massachusetts paper)*

Glamour photographer with own equipment and good contacts seeks sleeping or active partner. *(Advert in The Stage)*

WANTED – Solicitor, experienced in laundry or dye works, to drive wagon. *(Vancouver World)*

Donald's father told the court that his son's personality had completely changed since the accident. His career in the catering industry was finished because of it and he carried a chip on his shoulder.

Job Opportunities for Those with Earning Disabilities. *(South Manchester Reporter)*

COOK WANTED – March 1st. Comfortable room with radio; two in family; only one who can be well recommended. *(Advert in Hereford Paper)*

Lady with one child, two-and-a-half years old, seeks situation as housekeeper. oGod cook. *(Advert in S. African Paper)*

A brown snake bit reptile-collector Neville Burns, 19, in Sydney yesterday – and dropped dead. *(The People)*

WANTED URGENTLY – Male or Female serving person for top London nightclub. Must fit uniform 40" bust. *(New Evening Standard)*

Nursing sister Patricia Gregan had six double Scotches at a hotel and missed her train home. So she went by goods train – riding thirty miles astride the couplings between two trucks. Part of the ride was through a mile and a half long tunnel. Today in a Sydney court 54-year-old Mrs Gregan was charged with travelling on a portion of a goods train not intended for passengers and with being on railway property while intoxicated. She admitted both offences and was fined £200. Mrs Gregan said: 'It was a terrifying experience.' She promised she would not do it again. *(Daily Mail)*

Miss Georgina P. Mason, psychologist, quoted the case of a nine-year-old boy who ran amok with a hatchet in the large family of which he was a member, saying, 'There are far too many bairns here.' She showed how by psychological treatment he became completely adjusted and several years later was working a guillotine in a printer's establishment. *(Ross-shire Journal)*

Friends' Academy, Locust Valley, Long Island, Co-educational, with special opportunities for boys. *(Friend's Intelligencer)*

Girl wanted for petrol pump attendant. *(Advert in Oxford Mail)*

A circus man in Bor, Yugoslavia, who has already eaten more than 22,500 razor blades, a ton of brassware, cutlery, nuts, bolts and assorted ironware, has now bought himself a bus – which he intends to eat within the next two years. *(Sunday Mirror)*

Youth wanted – To train as Petrol Pump Attendant. 5-day week, Mon. to Sat., 9–6 p.m. Elderly man would suit. *(Bantry)*

RECREATION DEPARTMENT: Borough of Richmond Requires An Assistant Cemeteries Superintendent.

LAKER AIRWAYS – CABIN STAFF. Staff required for Gatwick Base. All applicants must be between 20 and 33 years of age. Height 5'4" to 5'10". Education GCSE standard. Must be able to swim. *(Luton Gazette)*

A new £2,500,000 sewage treatment works for Chipping Norton got under way on Monday when County Councillor Oliver Colston performed a brief inaugural ceremony. *(Oxford Journal)*

Part-time Job – An unexpected vacancy for a KNIFE THROW-ER'S ASSISTANT *(Milton Keynes Gazette)*

Some people are being overcharged on funeral costs, the Lord Mayor of Norwich, Mr Ralph Roe, told the city's Health Committee yesterday. 'Some people are being taken for a ride,' Mr Roe commented. *(Eastern Daily Press)*

Brief details regarding conditions of service are set out in the attached copy letter headed 'Walk Tall with the City of London Special Constabulary'. Members of staff who are interested should either call, write or telephone giving details of age, height and occupation to: Mr. K. Short, City of London Special Constabulary.

'I soon hope to offer body piercing and chiropody but I'm just trying to find my feet at the moment . . .' *(Dewsbury Reporter)*

It was thought that he might follow in his father's footsteps and become a butcher and slaughterer but he soon left and joined the 1st Battalion of the Middlesex Regiment. *(Wembley News)*

SERVANT GIRL WANTED for country surgeon's home. £130 per week and the use of Harmonium on Sundays. Plymouth sister preferred. *(Pulse)*

YOUNG POULTRY MAN – A young poultry man, who is keen to climb the tree and already knows his work, is required immediately in Southern Africa. A good salary is offered with free passage and housing, and, for a bachelor, a servant to boot. *(Poultry World)*

FALKLAND ISLANDS – There are vacancies for TWO CAMP TEACHERS in the Falkland Islands Education Department. Candidates must be unmarried men. *(Observer)*

H.M. PRISON WAKEFIELD require a SEMI-SKILLED LABOURER. An ability to erect small scaffolds will be an advantage. *(Pontefract & Castleford Express)*

Why is it, I wonder, that butchers always seem cheerful? It is not that their job is a particularly enviable one, for in cold weather meat must be very cold to handle. Maybe they get rid of any bad temper by bashing away with their choppers. *(Woman's Own)*

Wanted – Chambermaid in rectory. Love in, 200 dollars a month. *(US paper)*

Wanted: First class male waitress. Only qualified persons considered.

Wanted – Unmarried girls to pick fresh fruit and produce at night.

A young woman wants washing and cleaning daily. *(Toronto Times)*

Wanted – Men to take care of cows that do not smoke or drink.

Wanted – Mother's help. Peasant working conditions.

Wanted – Widower with school age children requires person to assume general housekeeping duties. Must be capable of contributing to the growth of the family.

Wanted – Preparer of food. Must be dependable, like the food business and be willing to get his hands dirty. *(Baltimore Sun)*

When I was a child, what I wanted to be when I was grown up was an invalid. *(Quentin Crisp)*

He's been on the dole so long he goes to the staff dances. *(Bobby Thompson)*

He had ambitions, at one time, to become a sex maniac, but he failed his practical. *(Les Dawson)*

A good farmer is nothing more nor less than a handy man with a sense of humus. *(E.B. White)*

My friend, the undertaker, the last person on earth to let me down.

A married man must love his wife but a navvy can have his pick. *(Max Miller)*

Have you ever fallen out of a patient? *(Groucho Marx to a tree surgeon)*

The reason why we can sell our antiques for less is because we buy them direct from the manufacturer. *(Antique dealer advertising in the Washington Times)*

CAREERS GRAFFITI

Yesterday I couldn't spell engineer.
Now I are one

You Can Tell A British Workman By His Hands . . .
- They are always in his pockets

6

Medicine

Mountains of beef and butter are hard to swallow.

Disadvantages of sexual reproduction: The majority of humans tend to mate with species of their own sort.

These colours are detected by colons in the eyes.

Each woman ought to examine her breast or any other abominations.

In arthritis joints may cease up.

The symptoms of influenza are similar to those of flu.

The immune system is easily weekend.

People with diabetes must take insulin everyday with a needle. Some people need multiple erections everyday for diabetes. Most people with diabetes learn to give themselves erections.

Signs and symptoms of arthritis: joints all rusty.

The parents can decide on whether to have children or not.

While in Accident and Emergency, she was examined, x-rated and then sent home.

The skin was moist and dry.

The patient was alert and unresponsive.

Rectal examination revealed an active thyroid.

She stated that she had been constipated most of her life until she got a divorce.

Madame Curie invented the radiator.

I saw your patient today and she is staying under the car of the consultant for physical therapy.

Examination of genitalia revealed he is circus sized.

The patient refused an autopsy.

The patient has no previous history of suicide.

She has no rigors or shaking but her husband says that she was very hot in bed last night.

On the second day the knee felt better and on the third it disappeared completely.

She is numb from her toes down.

To be a good nurse you must be completely sterile.

It is a misconception for pregnant women to believe that alcohol has no effect on the unborn foetus.

The leopard has black spots on its body which look like sores – those who catch sores get leprosy.

Human beings share a need of food, shelter and sex with lower animals.

MEDICINE PLUS

Specialist in women and other diseases. *(Doctor's clinic in Rome)*

Do not drive car or operate machinery *(On Boot's children's cough medicine)*

Widow In Bed With A Case Of Salmon *(Liverpool Echo)*

So I went to the doctor's and he said, 'You've got hypochondria.' I said, 'Not that as well.' *(Tim Vine)*

'Bodies in the garden are a plant,' says wife. *(Hong Kong Standard)*

IF YOU HAVE NOT HAD YOUR FLU SHOT THIS YEAR, ASK YOUR DOCTOR OR NURSE TO GET ONE. *(Notice in a hospital)*

TB or not TB, that is the congestion. *(Woody Allen)*

Transplant Man Dies – Dusan Vlaco, from Yugoslavia, the second-longest surviving heart transplant patient, has died in Los Angeles. He received the transplant on September 18th, 1698. *(Belfast Telegraph)*

To prevent contraception: wear a condominium.

RIB TICKLERS

I met a guy this morning who had a glass eye – he didn't tell me, it just came out in the conversation. *(Jerry Dennis)*

Doctor: I don't like the look of your husband.
Wife: I don't either, but he's good to the children.

I went to the doctor and I said, 'It hurts me when I do that.' He said, 'Well, don't do it.' *(Tommy Cooper)*

Doctor: You're going to live until you are eighty.
Patient: I am eighty.
Doctor: What did I tell you?

First you forget names, then you forget faces, then you forget to pull your zipper up, then you forget to pull your zipper down. *(Leo Rosenberg)*

She got her looks from her father – he's a plastic surgeon. *(Groucho Marx)*

The doctor called the plumber out late on Saturday night because his lavatory cistern was not flushing. The plumber took two aspirins out of his pocket and put them down the toilet. When the doctor protested, the plumber said, 'You know the routine – if it's no better in the morning, give me a call.'

I got the bill for my surgery. Now I know why those doctors were wearing masks. *(J. Boren)*

Doctor: I'm afraid you're dying.
Patient: How long have I got?
Doctor: Ten . . .

Patient: Ten what? Ten weeks, ten days?
Doctor: Ten, nine, eight, seven . . .

A man went to the doctor's with a cucumber in his left ear, a carrot in his right ear and a banana up his nose. 'What's wrong with me?' he asked. 'Simple,' said the doctor, 'You're not eating properly.'

A woman went to the doctor's clutching the side of her face. 'What seems to be the problem?' asked the doctor. 'Well,' said the woman, removing her hand, 'it's this pimple on my cheek. There's a small tree growing from it, and a table and chairs, and a picnic basket. What on earth can it be?' 'It's nothing to worry about,' said the doctor. 'It's only a beauty spot.'

Medical Officer: How are your bowels working?
Recruit: Haven't been issued with any sir.
M.O.: I mean are you constipated?
Recruit: No, sir, I volunteered.
M.O.: For goodness sake man, don't you know the King's English.
Recruit: No, sir, is he?

MEDICAL GRAFFITI

DOCTORS' LOUNGE
– and they get paid for it
(St Thomas's hospital, London)

Is a Buddhist Monk refusing an injection at the dentist's trying to transcend dental medication?

AMNESIA RULES, O . . .

Give blood – play hockey

MEDICAL TERMINOLOGY – CHILDREN'S STYLE

Barium – What doctors do when their patients pass away

Bowel – A letter like A I O U

Caesarean Section – A neighbourhood in Rome

Coma – Punctuation mark

Dilate – Live longer

Fibula – A small lie

Genital – Not a Jew

Impotent – Distinguished, well-known

Morbid – A higher offer

Rectum – Dang nearly killed 'em

Varicose – Nearby

Vein – conceited

7

Some Strange Translations
At Home And Abroad

Sometimes the use of inappropriate English translations for various products and instructions results in some bizarre offerings:

French Creeps *(Crepes)*

Garlic Coffee *(Gaelic)*

Indonesian Nazi Goreng

Muscles of Marines

Lobster Thermos

Pork with fresh garbage *(cabbage)*

Prawn cock and tail

Roasted Duck let loose *(Free Range Duck)*

French fried ships *(chips)*

Strawberry Crap

Fresh caut soul

Sweat from the trolley

Teppan Yaki – Before your cooked right eyes

Toes with butter and jam

Hen Soop Soap of the day

Melon and prostitute hams

Eyes cream

Coffee Eggspress

Little Kids – Roasted or at spit

Lemon jews

Irish Stew a L'Ecossaise

Cock in wine/Lioness cutlet *(Coq au vin/Lyonnaise cutlet)*

Dreaded veal cutlet with potatoes in cream *(Breaded . . .)*

This week's speciality – MULES MARINERE

Our wines leave you nothing to hope for *(Switzerland Hotel)*

When translated into Chinese, the Kentucky Fried Chicken slogan 'finger-lickin' good' came out as 'eat your fingers off'.

Outside a Hong Kong tailor's shop: 'Ladies may have a fit upstairs'.

Colgate introduced a toothpaste in France called 'Cue', the name of a notorious pornographic magazine.

The genuine antics in your room come from our family castle. *(In a Bed & Breakfast in France)*

Special cocktails for the ladies with nuts. *(In a Tokyo bar)*

Please to bathe inside the tub. *(In a Japanese hotel room)*

Stop – Drive Sideways. *(Diversion sign in Kyushi, Japan)*

Take one of our horse-driven city tours – we guarantee no miscarriages. *(In a Czechoslovakian tourist agency)*

In an effort to boost orange juice sales in England, a campaign was devised to extol the drink's eye-opening, pick-me-up qualities. Hence the slogan, 'Orange juice. It gets your pecker up'.

Visitors are expected to complain at the office between the hours of 9 and 11 a.m. daily. *(In a hotel in Athens)*

Salad a firm's own make; limpid red beet soup with cheesy dumplings in the form of a finger; roasted duck let loose; beef rashers beaten up in the country people's fashion. *(From a Polish hotel menu)*

Ford had a problem in Brazil when the Pinto flopped. The company found out that Pinto was Brazilian slang for 'tiny male genitals'. Ford pried all the nameplates off and substituted Corcel, which means horse.

Taiwan – the translation of the Pepsi slogan 'Come alive with the Pepsi Generation' came out as 'Pepsi will bring your ancestors back from the dead'.

Yugoslavia – in the Europa Hotel, in Sarajevo, you will find this message on every door: 'Guests should announce the abandonment of theirs rooms before 12 o'clock, emptying the room at the latest until 14 o'clock, for the use of the room before 5 at the arrival or after the 16 o'clock at the departure, will be billed as one night more.'

The lift is being fixed for the next day. During that time we regret that you will be unbearable. *(Bucharest)*

The flattening of underwear with pleasure is the job of the chambermaid. *(Yugoslavia)*

You are invited to take advantage of the chambermaid. *(Japan)*

You are invited to visit the cemetery where famous Russians are buried daily. *(Russia)*

Not to perambulate the corridors in the hours of repose in the boots of ascension. *(Austria)*

Drop your trousers here for best results. *(Bangkok cleaners)*

Dresses for street walking. *(Paris dress shop)*

Because of the impropriety of entertaining guests of the opposite sex in the bedroom, it is suggested that the lobby be used for this purpose. *(Zurich)*

Teeth extracted by the latest Methodists. *(Hong Kong dentist)*

Ladies, leave your clothes here and spend the afternoon having a good time. *(Rome laundry)*

It is forbidden to enter a woman even a foreigner dressed as a man. *(Bangkok Temple)*

We take your bags and send them in all directions. *(Copenhagen Airport)*

If this is your first visit to the USSR, you are welcome to it. *(in a Moscow hotel)*

Our nylons cost more than common, but you'll find they are best in the long run. *(Tokyo shop)*

Customers giving orders will be promptly executed. *(Notice in Bombay tailor's)*

Haircutting while you wait. *(Dublin Barber's)*

Please do not lock the door as we have lost the key. *(St David's School)*

The best place in town to take a leak. *(Outside a radiator repair shop)*

We are closed on Labour Day. *(Outside a maternity clothes shop)*

To stop the drip, turn cock to the right. *(In a Finnish washroom)*

No children allowed. *(In a Florida maternity ward)*

No trespassing. Violators will be prosecuted – Sisters of Mercy. *(On a gate outside a convent)*

La orquesta ejecuto el 'Good sabe the Queen', *coreado por la concurencia, lo mismo que el* 'Forisa Folley good fillow'. *(La Nacion, Buenos Aires)*

Push Push. *(On the door of a maternity hospital)*

Closed due to illness. *(In a health shop window)*

Please knock loudly – bell out of order. *(On electrical repair shop door)*

Don't sleep with a drip – call your plumber. *(On a plumber's van)*

Closing down – thanks to all our customers. *(Outside a shop)*

Do not leave this restaurant without sampling the tart of this house. *(Swiss restaurant)*

Our curries are so delicious you will repeat often. *(Manchester restaurant)*

CHICKEN TIKKA £2.00
Homeless chicken marinated in yoghurt and spices then baked
(Megna takeaway menu, Narbeth)

But sometimes it isn't easy to make yourself understood, even in England.

The appetising smell of chips drew us to a Chinese restaurant at Penrith. We hadn't much time so I asked an immaculate waiter if we could 'carry out'. He looked puzzled. I tried again, speaking very slowly. Did they have 'carry-outs'? 'Ah,' he said, brightening, 'We have chicken curry rice. But we do not have curry oot.' We laughed all the rest of the way to Blackpool. *(The Sunday Post)*

8

A Register of Names

From time to time parents, despite the best of intentions, give their children names that might well plague them unto death (or alteration by deed poll). In the main, horror combinations of Christian and surname are self-evident to those remotely worldly wise, but clearly some parents do not fit into that category. Here are some names that contributors swear are genuine. Most are patently obvious, but occasionally the imagination needs to be used:

Russell Sprout; Teresa Green; Orson Cart; Walter Wall; Rose Plant; Rick O'Shay; Ben Trotter; Sam Barr; Al Kaholic; Anita Bath; Annie Boddy; April Showers; Barbara Wire; Barry Abone; Bell E. Flopp; Di Rhea; Duane Pipe; Eileen Downe; Jack Cass; Joanna Hooker; Lou Tennant; Nick Carrs; Pat McGroin; R. Sole; Thomas Gunn; Justin Case; Alan Quay; Ben Arnner; Christopher Wave; Cybil Wrights; Dennis Elbow; Dusty Rhodes; Ed Turner; Fiona Friend; Gordon Nomes; Helen Back; Hugo First; Isla White; Anne Teak; C. Senor; Gail Storm; Jack Hammer; Jo King; Lee King; Neil Downe; Penny Lane; Rick Shaw; Sally Forth; Warren Peace; Seymour Butts; Joe King; Norman Gates.

Canadian typist Chamber Landis, 23, has often had her leg pulled about her unusual Christian name. But it will be worse now. She has just married Vancouver salesman Les Potts. *(Tit-Bits)*

Gnanasamunthamurthi Naicker intends to change his name to Gnanasamunthamurthi Moodley, reports the Government Gazette Durban. *(The Evening News)*

The new chairman of the Leicester Swimming Club is Mr Ivor Finn. *(Leicester Mercury)*

Boxing champion George Foreman named his first son 'George' after himself – an arrangement with which Foreman was so pleased that he also gave the name to his second son. In fact, Foreman soon had five sons – all named George.

A journalist from *The Times* requested information to be sent by post. Asked for her name by the telephonist she replied, 'Catherine – with a C – Riley'. Next day she received an envelope addressed to: 'Catherine Withersea Riley'.

After eight years' searching the Parish Register for a name to match the initials H.W.P. on a stone slab in his church, teacher Phillip Randall, of Eye, near Peterborough, has solved the mystery. The initials stand for Hot Water Pipe. *(Sunday Mirror)*

O. Howe Good worked in the Complaints Department for the New York Telephone Company in 1931.

Two bathroom fitters employed, at the same time, by Prestige Fitments in the 1950s were named Les Hot and Les Cool.

A man called Jack Frost sold refrigerators in Washington, D.C. in the 1930s.

Also in Washington, D.C., in 1941 a milkman I.M. Wiser was married to May B. Wiser.

A.C. Current was an electrical contractor in Tontogany, Ohio. His son's name was D.C. Current.

In 1938 Miss Birdie Snyder married Mr C. Canary to become Birdie Canary.

Despite her name, Iona Fiddle of St Paul, Minnesota, never did.

In the 1940s an American, William Williams, lived on Williams Street, in Williamsburg, Kansas.

Atta Atta was an immigrant from Ata, in Atica, Greece.

Virginia Hight became librarian for the Virginia Heights school in Roanoke.

Other unusual American names:

I.M.A. Balmer was a funeral director; the Clipper brothers were barbers; A. Ball was a pitcher from Illinois; Cali Fornia came from San Pedro, California; Iccolo Miccolo played a piccolo in the Los Angeles Philharmonic Orchestra in 1935; and the school dentist for the Burlington Independent School District was Dr H.A. Toothacre.

Then there was Nina Clock from Minnesota; Dina Might from Michigan; Alma Mater from Tulsa; Deep C. Fisher from San Francisco; Twinkle Starr from Portland, Oregon; and B.A. Crank from Arkansas.

Comic names have rarely coincided with football success. Harry Daft won five England caps, but Segar Bastard was shunned after one. Brazil's Rafael Scheidt was a self-fulfilling prophesy at Celtic. Daniel Killer, the Argentine defender of the 1970s, was kind to children and animals. And Australian goalkeeper Norman Conquest is merely a footnote in history. *('Clogger' from the Guardian)*

At a formal sherry party at Oxford, a lady with the imposing name of Ironside-Bax saw Dr Spooner, whom she knew, in conversation with a professor she wished to meet. She accordingly approached Spooner and asked to be introduced. 'Certainly, dear lady,' said Spooner. 'Professor, I would like you to meet a friend of mine, Mrs Iron-Backside.' *(This Language of Ours – G. Culkin)*

Q: What's the difference between Tufnell Park and Florence?
A: In Tufnell Park there are lots of little girls called Florence, but there are no girls called Tufnell Park in Florence.

To think that these names from the 2005 National Register of Births will appear on school registers in the years to come!

General Choices

Apple, Misty Kid Spiteri, Pepper Coxon, Tullulah Lilac, Amberdori Sonny, Florian, Arlow, Blythe, Buster, Cookie, Rags, Ski, Paige, Bobby-Joe, Trixy Stretch, Courtney, Tyler, Baskerville, and finally, fashion stylist Katy England's son, Wolf.

Arthurian, Greek, and Roman Influence

Guinevere, Gawaine, Mungo, Isis, Titus, Ulrich, Solomon and Elwood.

Naming after a Plant

Lily, Fleur, Indigo, Poppy, Daisy, Sky, Tiger, Blossom and Dandelion.

Something Aquatic

Dolphin, Pearl and Ocean.

The Age of the Blitz

Sid, Stan, Ernie, Vic, Fred, Joe and Archie.

Brand and Consumer Appellations

Evian, Nike, Armani, more than 150 Chardonnays, Lexus, Versace, Chanel (commonly pronounced 'Channel').

IKEA Influenced?

Arjun, Aari, Han, Dann, Malaika and Emil.

Some names appear to have been misspelled, for example Alicia becomes Alisha, but can anyone decipher these?

Kaella, Chervanna, Kymia and Jaspin.

9

Mothers and Children

CHILDREN'S ADVICE

Never trust a dog to watch your food.

When you want something expensive, ask your grandparents.

Wear a hat when feeding seagulls.

Sleep in your clothes so you don't have to get dressed in the morning.

Never try to hide a piece of broccoli in your glass of milk.

Never flush the toilet when your Dad's in the shower.

Always say your mum's new hairstyle suits her if she asks you.

Never tell your mum that her diet is not working.

When you get a bad report always give it to your mum when she's on the phone.

Never try to dress a cat up as a baby.

Never spit into a strong wind when the rest of the family is behind you.

Never do a practical joke in a police station.

Never tell your brother that you are not going to do what your mother told you.

Remember you are never too old to hold your father's hand or give him a kiss.

Stay away from prunes and Brussels sprouts.

Only pay for a sea trip on the way back – if you don't come back, then you don't pay.

Bless Them – The Things they Say

Little Boy (from Bedroom): Dad, I'm thirsty. Can I have a drink of water?
Dad: No you can't. You had your chance.
Little Boy (after short pause): Dad, I'm still thirsty. Can I have a drink of water?
Dad: No, you can't, and if you ask again I'll have to give you a smack.
Little Boy (after a longer pause): Dad, when you come in to give me a smack, can I have a drink of water?

According to a radio report, a middle school in Oregon was faced with a unique problem. A lot of girls were beginning to use lipstick and would put it on in the girls' toilets. After applying it, they would press their lips to the mirror, leaving dozens of little lip prints.

Finally the principal decided that something had to be done. She called all the girls to the toilets and met them there with the caretaker. She explained that all these lip prints were causing a major problem for him when he had to clean the mirrors every night. To demonstrate how difficult it was to clean the mirrors, she asked the caretaker to show them how he had to do it. He took out a long-handled squeegee, dipped it in a toilet, and then cleaned the mirror with it. Since then there have been no lip prints on the mirrors.

'Why were you absent from school yesterday?' the class teacher asked a five-year-old? 'I went to see Heavenly Angel,' said the lad. 'Oh, is that a new film?' she asked. 'No, Miss,' he replied. 'It's my new baby sister.'

A teacher was sitting at her desk grading papers, when her class came back from lunch. Alice informed her, 'Paul has to go to the principal's office.' 'I wonder why,' the teacher mused. 'Because he's a following person,' Alice replied. 'A what?' the teacher asked.

'It came over the loudspeaker: "The following persons are to go to the office . . ."'

A wise schoolteacher sent this note to all parents on the first day of school: 'If you promise not to believe everything your child says happens at school, I'll promise not to believe everything they say happens at home.'

After putting her children to bed, a mother changed into old slacks and a droopy blouse and proceeded to wash her hair. As she heard the children getting more and more rumbustious, her patience grew thin. At last she threw a towel around her head and stormed into their room, putting them back to bed with stern warnings. As she left the room, she heard her three-year-old say with a trembling voice, 'Who was that?'

A new neighbour asked the little girl next door if she had any brothers and sisters. She replied, 'No, I'm the lonely child.'

First Boy: Should I cut the pizza into four?
Second Boy: No, I'm really hungry – cut it into six.

The child was a typical four-year-old girl – cute, inquisitive, bright as a new penny. When she expressed difficulty in grasping the concept of marriage, her father decided to pull out the wedding photo album, thinking visual images would help. One page after another, he pointed out the bride arriving at the church, the entrance, the wedding ceremony, the reception, etc.

'Now do you understand?' he asked.

'I think so,' she said. 'Is that when Mammy came to work for us?'

When one of the pupils in the Infants became ill with chicken pox, the teacher asked if anyone else had ever had chicken pox. After a while a little lad raised his hand and said, 'No, Miss, but I have had Coco-Pops.'

Out shopping, the patience of a mother with three little girls and a baby was wearing thin as all the girls persisted in calling out 'Mammy . . . Mammy'. Finally, in exasperation the mother said, 'I don't want to hear the word "Mammy" for at least five minutes.'

A few seconds went by, then one girl tugged on her Mum's skirt and said, 'Excuse me, miss.'

A very dirty little lad came in from playing in the yard and asked his mother, 'Who am I?' Ready to play the game, she said, 'I don't know! Who are you?'

'Wow!' cried the child. 'Mrs Johnson was right. She said I was so dirty, my own mother wouldn't recognise me!'

The pub/restaurant where the mother had taken her two sons for a meal was crowded with fans watching a football match on television. The harassed waitress took the order, but more than half an hour passed without any sign of her return, and the mother was having difficulty keeping her children entertained. Suddenly, shouts of a goal came from the bar. 'Hey,' shouted the eleven-year-old, 'it sounds as if someone's just been served.'

Several years ago, a father returned home from a trip just when a storm hit, with crashing thunder and severe lightning. As he entered the bedroom at about 2 a.m., he found his two children in bed with his wife because they had been scared, so he resigned himself to sleeping in the spare room that night.

The next day, he talked to the children, and explained that it was OK for them to sleep with their mother when the storm was bad, but when he was expected home, he would be grateful if they would stay in their own rooms. After his next trip several weeks later, his wife and children went to pick him up at the airport. Since the plane was late, everyone had come into the terminal to wait for the plane's arrival, along with hundreds of other folks waiting for their arriving passengers.

As he entered the waiting area, his four-year-old son saw him, and came running, calling at the top of his voice, 'Dad, Dad, I've got some good news. Nobody slept with Mum while you were away this time.'

While taking a routine vandalism report at a Junior School, a policewoman was interrupted by a little girl of about five. Looking up and down at her uniform, the girl asked, 'Are you a policewoman?'

'Yes,' the policewoman answered.

'My mother said if I ever needed help I had to ask the police. Is that right?'

The policewoman confirmed this. 'Well, then,' said the little girl as she extended her foot toward the policewoman, 'would you please tie my shoelace?'

While working for an organisation that delivers lunches to the elderly, a lady used to take her four-year-old daughter on her afternoon rounds. The little girl was always intrigued by the various appliances of old age, particularly the canes, walkers and wheelchairs. One day the lady found her staring at a pair of false teeth soaking in a glass. As she braced herself for the inevitable barrage of questions, her daughter merely turned and whispered, 'The tooth fairy will never believe this.'

A little girl became restless as the preacher's sermon dragged on and on. Finally, she leaned over to her mother and whispered, 'Mammy, if we give him the money now, will he let us go?'

A six-year-old was overheard reciting the Lord's Prayer at a church service: 'And forgive us our trash passes as we forgive those who passed trash against us.'

A mother took her three-year-old daughter to church for the first time. The lights were lowered, and the choir began processing down the aisle, carrying lighted candles. All was quiet until the little one started singing in a loud voice, 'Happy birthday to you, happy birthday to you . . .'

A Sunday School teacher asked her class why Joseph and Mary took Jesus with them to Jerusalem. After a long pause, a small child replied, 'Was it because they couldn't find a baby-sitter?'

A mother was teaching her three-year-old the Lord's Prayer. For several evenings at bedtime she repeated it after her mother. One night she said she wanted to say it by herself. The mother listened with pride as she carefully pronounced each word, right up to the end of the prayer. 'Lead us not into temptation,' she prayed, 'but deliver us some e-mail, Amen.'

Mum, I'll always love you, but I'll never forgive you for cleaning my face with spit on a hanky.

A granny was teaching her eight-year-old granddaughter how to sew. After she had gone through a lengthy explanation of how to thread the machine, the little girl stepped back, put her hands on her hips, and said in disbelief, 'You mean you can do all that, but you can't operate my Game Boy?'

A little girl was diligently pounding away on her grandfather's word processor. She told him she was writing a story. 'What's it about?' he asked. 'I don't know,' she replied. 'I can't read yet, can I?'

MOTHER'S ADVICE AND SAYINGS

Wait till your father gets home.

When you get to my age, then you'll understand.

Don't worry, it could have been a lot worse.

You might think it's not cold, but I know you need a sweater.

Look at me when I'm talking to you.

Get your elbows off the table.

Don't stare; it's not polite.

Don't worry, you're small now but you'll shoot up.

Don't interrupt.

Because I said so.

Not while you're under my roof.

Just because everyone else does it doesn't mean you have to.

When you fall off that swing and break your leg, don't come running to me.

If you don't eat your vegetables you'll never grow up.

Eat your crusts – it'll make you hair curly.

You're just like your father.

I'll kiss it and make it better.

Nobody ever said life was fair.

Wipe that grin off your face.

Don't slouch.

Go and ask your father.

Don't raise your voice to me.

You should have thought about that before we left the house.

Don't talk with your mouth full.

You'll grow into it.

Eat it – it's good for you.

Don't sit too close to the TV – you'll ruin your eyes.

There's nothing else until you finish your dinner.

How many times do I have to tell you?

It looks like a bomb has gone off in this room.

You're not going to wear THAT, are you?

What have you done with your hair?

No sweets – you'll not eat your dinner.

Take your shoes off in the house.

Close the door – were you born in a field?

Turn that music down.

Make sure you wear clean underwear, in case you're in an accident.

Keep laughing and I'll give you something to cry about.

You'll sit there until all that spinach is eaten.

If I've told you once, I've told you a million times – don't exaggerate.

Just remember how lucky you are – there are millions starving in Africa.

And some final advice for mothers — if you have a lot of tension and you get a headache, do what it says on the aspirin bottle: 'Take two and keep away from children.'

QUESTIONS CHILDREN ASK

Why do clocks go clockwise?

Why do Kamikaze pilots wear helmets?

If one synchronised swimmer drowns, do the rest have to drown too?

If you are born again, do you have two belly buttons?

When cheese gets its photo taken, what does it say?

Why isn't there mouse-flavoured cat food?

How can you have free gifts when all gifts are free?

What does God say when somebody in Heaven sneezes?

Do they sterilise the needles for lethal injections?

What should you do if you see an endangered animal eating an endangered plant?

What do you plant to grow a seedless melon?

How can there be self-help groups?

Do those crisscross screwdrivers belong to Philip?

Why doesn't superglue stick to the tube?

If dolphins are so clever, why is it they're always getting caught in nets?

Why do 'fat chance' and 'slim chance' mean the same thing?

Why do people say, 'It's always in the last place you look' when of course it is?

If a rabbit's foot is so lucky, what happened to the rabbit?

Why do joggers never smile?

If man evolved from apes why is it that we still have them?

What's the speed of dark?

What's another word for 'synonym'?

How does the man who drives the snowplough get to work?

Why don't they make aeroplanes out of the same material as the black box?

Why do mothers take their children to the supermarket to smack them?

How do 'Do not walk on the grass' signs get there?

Why doesn't the wool on sheep shrink when it rains?

What was the best thing before sliced bread?

Why do men have nipples?

Why doesn't Tarzan have a beard?

Can you cry underwater?

When speaking on behalf of the silent majority, how come anyone knows what to say?

10

School–Home Communications

EXCUSES – SCHOOL AND HOMEWORK

I did not do my homework because you ASKED me to do it and did not TELL me to do it – I thought it was optional.

My son will not be attending for a while because we have decided to send him off to Switzerland to military school for a couple of days, but don't worry, he will return a perfect gentleman.

Elizabeth cannot hand in her homework because she forgot it.

John was off school yesterday because the whole family had just flown all the way from Florida and we all were very tired.

Please excuse Joan from Jim today – she is administrating.

Please excuse Martin from P.E. Yesterday he fell out of a tree and misplaced his hip.

Carlos was absent yesterday because he was playing football and was hurt in the growing part.

Raymond was off school yesterday because he had very loose vowels.

Irving was absent because he missed his bust.

Sean has not been to school because he says he is frightened. I have told him that he should take the bull between the teeth and get himself there.

Robbie was off school because he had a cold and could not breed easily.

Roseanne was in bed with gramps yesterday.

Thompson has to go to the hospital today for x-rays. The doctor thinks he might have broken his spatula and collarbone.

My son is ill and should not take P.E. today – please execute him.

Angela was off yesterday because we took her to McDonald's and the food made her delirious.

Al was not in school yesterday because he did not feel like going.

My son Michael won't be in school today because he caught his thing in his zipper this morning while dressing and is in a lot of pain.

Please excuse Henry for being late but he was stuck in the bathroom without any toilet paper.

Please excuse my son for being absent but he was bad with the flue.

I'm sorry Tyler was off school yesterday but his hormones were raging.

Emily will not be at school today as she coming with me to take her mother to hospital who is having her overtures out.

The children have been off school because there is a lot of measles about and I have had them humanised.

Darren has been off school because he said he had a bad stomach but the doctor says it's all in his head and that he is a hypodermic.

Mary has been off school helping me because I have been in bed under the doctor and it has done me no good and if there is no improvement I am going to get another doctor.

Thor is late because I had to take him to the dentist. His teeth on the top are all right but the ones on his bottom are really hurting him.

Aaron will not be in today. Last night we had an accident in the kitchen when my cooker backfired and blew my knob off.

Joseph fell out of a tree last night and today has a pane in his leg.

Billy is in bed with swellings in his throat and the doctor says it is the gathering of the clans.

LETTERS TO SCHOOL

Dear Headteacher . . .

William pulled the chain on the toilet and the box fell on his head.

I thought you should know that my husband is a diabetic and has to take insulin regular but finds he is lethargic to it.

I will not be able to pay the dinner money this week as I have fallen into errors with my landlord and milkman.

In accordance with your letter I have given birth to twins in the enclosed envelope.

I am very annoyed that you have branded my son illiterate. This is a lie as I married his father a week before he was born.

I am sorry I forgot to put down the names of all of my children because of contraceptional difficulties.

Joanne's grandfather had to go to hospital this morning after he had put his foot through a hole in his back passage.

Arthur already holds black belt grades in Judo and Karate, so this award makes him a leading marital arts practitioner in Rotherham.

Please could you do something about your older pupils who are continually banging their balls against my fence on the way home from school.

SCHOOL REPORTS

A science teacher described one hapless pupil as 'chemically inert'.

The propensity of William to project himself into another world is unlikely to help him master the geography of this one. *(Geography)*

He has worked entirely to his own satisfaction.

If ignorance is bliss, this boy is in for a life of undiluted happiness.

Ronald should go far – however, I am not sure in which direction.

Craig has a fertile imagination but I am not happy that he has taken Stalin as his role model. *(History)*

Mary's cookery skills are developing well but I do think her plans to set up a tapas bar, with your support, could be a bit ambitious. *(Home Economics)*

While Charles did obtain 93% in his GCSE Spanish, I do think his revision of the past subjunctive needs to be more thorough.

Samantha keeps pestering me with the question of the value of a 'dead language', however her own lack of life could well prove terminal for the subject. *(Latin)*

I have spent more time on Frederick's homework than he has.

The problem with Jane 'hiding her light under a bushel' for so long is that I worry it might have gone out.

Since my last report, Rachel has reached rock bottom and is starting to dig.

Sean's progress in Design Technology is faltering – the gates are down, the lights are flashing, but the train is not coming.

His main stumbling block is the one in his head.

The longest I've known for something to stay in her head is one hour – and that was a cold.

One of his good points is that he stops to think about everything – one of his bad ones is that he has to be reminded to start again.

John is to Design Technology what Attila the Hun was to pacifism.

Charles is trying in Maths – very.

11

Overheard in the Playground

If the great and the good can be relied upon to give us the benefit of bloopers, then it comes as no surprise that the playground location can be a source of entertaining examples.

He said I had class . . . with a capital 'K'.

The teacher asked me if I was at the school for good – I told her I wasn't there for good.

The policeman told me that he had read I had been injured in the tabloids – I told him it was not anywhere near the tabloids.

Brave men run in our family.

Everyday I was up before the crack of noon.

There were these sheep, gazing on almost vertical slopes

First girl: What's his job then?
Second girl: He keeps saying he's a man of letters because he works for the Post Office.

My Aunt says children should be obscure and not heard.

He had to use biceps to deliver the baby.

First boy: Permit? What's a permit?
Second boy: You know – Permit the frog.

Teacher: You're in school very early today, George.
George: Yes, sir, my form teacher has been complaining about my punctuation.

A mother sees off her son with the words, 'I don't want you talking to those naughty boys. I'm not having any fratricide here.'

It lasted from here to maternity.

Let's get down to the brass roots.

She's changed her name by flagpole.

First girl: I spy something beginning with L.
Second girl: Alarm?

My Dad's Hungarian and even though he can speak English, I wouldn't say he was fluorescent.

This is like déjà vu all over again.

You can observe a lot just by watching.

He must have made that before he died.

I knew I was going to get the wrong bus so I left early.

Cricket is 90% mental – the other half is physical.

First pupil: What time is it?
Second pupil: Do you mean now?

When you come to a fork in the road, take it.

I made a wrong mistake.

Don't look a gift Norse in the mouth.

If you want plastic surgery on your face then it's no skin off my nose.

I saw part of it all the way through.

If I look confused it's because I'm thinking.

They should have stood closer apart.

It really gets my dandruff up.

She was made a sheepgoat of.

They said the wall was destroyed after being attacked by the elephants . . . I mean the elements.

Q: What do you call a Frenchman in sandals?
A: Philippe Philoppe.

Either come with me . . . or we go together.

Was yesterday the 31st of February?

I told my Granny her stockings were wrinkled but the trouble was she wasn't wearing any.

Were you here on Tuesday? The smell was awful.

When my brother quarrels, he goes historical.

I told the teacher I could hardly hear in assembly this morning. She said it was because of the agnostics in the hall.

If they are going to introduce the Euro, I think they should wait until the old people are dead.

First boy: What's the name of that famous woman with the lamp?
Second boy: Aladdin?

Then there are the putdowns. Children can be very cruel . . .

His mother gives him a see-through lunch-box so that he can tell whether he's on his way from school or to school.

He'd have difficulty counting to twenty if he hadn't learned how to take off his shoes.

You know how some monks take a vow of silence, well she's taken a vow of talking.

And finally, the trade secret . . .

I don't really like dressing this way, but it stops my parents from dragging me with them everywhere they go. *(Teenager, with nose rings, baggy clothing and spiked hair, to a friend)*

12

School Matters

HEAD TEACHER BLOOPERS

Don't let worry kill you – let the school help.

Because of the large number of examinations in the hall today, children will be examined at both ends.

Remember to offer your prayers for the many who are sick of our school community.

After assembly on Thursday afternoon there will be a Year 6 ice-cream party. Would Miss Thomas, Mrs Franklin and Mrs George, who are providing the milk, please meet at lunch time.

Because Sunday is Easter Day, Sophie Briggs from Form 8D will come onto the stage and lay an egg on the table.

A 'Beans and Sausage' supper will take place in the hall on Thursday and this will be followed by music.

Mr Evans, the head teacher, spoke briefly, much to the delight of his audience.

Years 9,10 and 11 will be presenting 'Hamlet' next Friday in the school hall and all pupils are encouraged to buy tickets at the office for this tragedy.

In a word – I don't think so.

I would like to thank all of you children for your prayers for the recovery of our deputy head Mrs Hall – God is good, Mrs Hall is better.

The head of the PTA gave the school secretary the list of prizes for the raffle to be typed and amongst the list was the item 'large cans of lager'. The secretary gave the list to the head teacher who asked, 'What happened to the large candelabra?'

If you can't imitate him, then don't copy him.

For your information, just answer me one question.

I'm willing to admit that I may not always be right, but I'm never wrong.

Secretary: Should I destroy these ten-year-old records?
Head teacher: Yes, but make copies.

True, I have taken a long time to give you a 'yes' or 'no' – but now I'm giving you a definite maybe.

Never make forecasts about the future.

Put it out of your mind – soon it will be a forgotten memory.

Who is sitting in the empty chair?

We note with regret that Mrs Calhoun is recuperating from an automobile accident.

In the Sixth Form we've been trying to get uniform done away with. I think we'll soon be down to the boys just wearing a tie and the girls a grey skirt.

Ladies who have kindly undertaken to act as school crossing wardens are reminded again that if they attempt to carry out their duties without their clothing on motorists are unlikely to take any notice of them. *(Circular to school parents)*

Mr. E.G. Winterton, head teacher, would not comment on the threat. However, he did say, 'Some children have been behaving very childishly.' *(Doncaster Post)*

Today was the first day for nine days that some pupils have been able to use their toilets. We must do something to relieve this situation. *(From the head teacher's report to governors)*

Teachers who wish to have typing done should take advantage of the female staff in the main office.

I would like to remind staff that I shall take as long as is required to make a snap decision.

The after-lunch talk was given by Mr Derek Wigram – school head teacher, retired, but now serving the Lord in an advisory capacity. *(Crusade)*

Winners in the Parents' Association home-made wine competition were Mrs Davis (fruity, well-rounded), Mrs Raynor (fine colour and full-bodied), and Miss Ogle- Smith (slightly acid, but should improve if laid down). *(Head teacher's circular)*

The head teacher of King James' School will preach at the Parish Church on Sunday, May 13th, and another of the staff on May 6th. On both these Sundays I hope to be away on holiday. *(Vicar's announcement in St Mary the Virgin's parish newsletter)*

Will those teachers wishing for leave of absence to attend the funeral of a grandmother or other close relative please inform the Head before 12 noon on the day of the match.

The head teacher said that they still had piles to deal with. *(Staff circular re: exam papers)*

I know you believe you understand what you think I said, but I am not sure you realise that what you heard is not what I meant. *(Head teacher at staff meeting)*

Will the individual who borrowed a ladder from the caretaker last month kindly return same immediately, otherwise further steps will be taken. *(Head teacher's request to staff in Derbyshire)*

Comments from references from head teachers:

Mr Bingham has worked for me for fifteen years and when he left I was perfectly satisfied.

If you can get Mr George to work for you, you will indeed be fortunate.

And observations from CVs received by head teachers:

My intensity and focus are at inordinately high levels, and my ability to complete projects on time is unspeakable.

Education: Curses in liberal arts, curses in computer science, curses in accounting.

Personal: Married, 1992 Chevrolet.

I have an excellent track record, although I am not a horse.

I am a rabid typist.

Proven ability to track down and correct erors.

Personal interests: Donating blood. 15 gallons so far.

References: None, I've left a path of destruction behind me.

Strengths: Ability to meet deadlines while maintaining composer.

Don't take the comments of my former employer too seriously, they were unappreciative beggars and slave drivers.

Extensive background in accounting. I can also stand on my head!

And from the covering letter . . .

Thank you for your consideration. Hope to hear from you shorty.

And if you make it as far as the interview . . .

The young teacher was asked at his interview what particular role he had played as 'Local co-ordinator of regional media distribution', a post he had included in his CV. 'To be perfectly honest,' he replied, 'for a couple of years I was Head Paper Boy.'

In the interview they put me up against a woman and it was a case of touch and go.

STAFF GRAFFITI

Our Headteacher has shoes so shiny I can see my face in them

The wages of sin is death but the wages here are a lot worse

SCHOOL MATTERS IN PRINT

MEDINA TO HAVE PARENT TEACHER ASSASSINA-TION *(Headline in Medina Sentinel)*

Councillor Mrs Hallinan said the education authority had set up various nits in different parts of Cardiff. *(South Wales Echo)*

John Fisher, the student star of St George's College Christmas concert, was in a car accident last week. However, we are happy to state that he will still be able to appear this evening in four pieces. *(Durham Advertiser)*

Formerly a don at Oxford, he developed later an interest in education, and migrated to Ontario. *(Canadian Review)*

The winner of St Patrick's competition to guess the number of sweets in the jar was Mrs Linden, who will therefore travel to Majorca by air, spend five days in a luxury hotel (all inclusive) and fly home via Paris, without any need to spend a penny. *(Announcement in a Westmoreland church magazine)*

Nineteen-year-old Texan student Roger Martinez set a world record by swallowing 225 live goldfish in 42 minutes in a San Antonio contest. His prize: a free fish dinner. *(Sun)*

The nearest school is over five miles away in one direction and practically twelve miles in the opposite direction. *(Ulster Magazine and Eire Review)*

Apart from an isolated incident of violence in 1470 when the dean of the faculty of arts was shot at with bows and arrows, and if one glosses over the Jacobite demonstrations of 1715, the university has been singularly free of student unrest. *(From prospectus of St Andrew's University)*

The first hearing was adjourned to enable the students to be regally represented. *(Surrey Advertiser)*

Martin C—, aged 63, a retired teacher, was said by a police officer at Clerkenwell, last week, to have walked along Randolph Road, Camden Town, 'absolutely nude' on Sunday afternoon, shouting: 'How about this, then?' *(North London Press)*

These are some of the pictures on show at the Young Artists' Exhibition in Moscow's Central Exhibition Hall, one of the USSR's 50th Anniversary events. The 1,500 exhibits, displayed to the best advantage over nearly two acres, are the pick of 20,000 submitted by young painters, graphic artists and sculptors in every Soviet Republic. Nearly all were executed over the past two years. *(Soviet Weekly)*

Mr Wedgwood Benn said: '. . . there is a great revolution under way in education. My education policy is to raise the school leaving age to 65.' *(Evening Post)*

Letters from The Times:

Sir,

I possess an unused pre-stamped postcard that was issued to me when I first went to camp as a member of the Boys' Brigade in 1943. Headed 'CAMP (labour saving) POST CARD' it incorporates a 'tick or delete' list which included:

Dear Mum/Dad/Uncle/Aunt/Old Thing;

I am . . . In the pink/In clink/Having a gorgeous time/Starving/Home sick.

The weather is . . . Fine/Wet/Below zero/Tropical.

My money is . . . Spent/Given to charity/In the canteen/Have plenty.

Please send me . . . A clean shirt/Nourishing food/A return ticket/Your love.

Camp is . . . Wonderful/Horrible/Going too quickly/Not 'arf alright.

Your loving . . . Son/Nephew/Pal.

Sir,

To get your offspring to communicate when they are away, write to them, ending the letter: 'I hope the enclosed cheque is of some use', but without enclosing anything.

You will get a phone call the next day.

Sir,

Our understanding daughter had a rubber stamp made for her younger brother when he was at university. It read: 'Date as postmark. Dear Mum and Dad. Still alive. All is well. Love George.'

SCHOOL GRAFFITI

WET PAINT
This is <u>not</u> an instruction!

The Graffiti in this school is terrible – and so are the dinners

Examinations - Natures Laxative
(London Poly.)

Education kills by degrees
(Newcastle University)

Don't let them cut hire education
(Camberwell School)

Road safety notice outside of Junior School:
Drive carefully. Don't kill a child.
Wait for a teacher

13

Some Unusual Scholarships and Awards

In the United States, there is an abundance of scholarships made available by different types of organisations. Most of these, as in Britain, are awarded for traditional subjects such as Languages, Music, Art, etc., but a substantial number fall into a category that might be considered 'unusual', or even bizarre.

Scholarships for Left-Handed Students. $1,000 available to left-handed students to attend Juniata College.

Duck Brand Duct Tape Stuck On Prom Contest. Open to students aged fourteen or over who are attending a high school prom this spring. Entrants must enter as a couple (two individuals) and attend a high school prom wearing complete attire and accessories made from duct tape. The submission must include a photo of the couple together. First prize is $2,500 for each member of the winning couple and $2,500 for the school hosting the prom. The winning couple will be selected based on a variety of criteria, including originality, workmanship, quantity of duct tape used, use of colours and creative use of accessories.

Scholar Athlete Milk Moustache of the Year. Candidates must demonstrate excellence in academics, athletic performance, leadership and community service. There is one scholarship of $7,500 to each of the regional winners.

SPAACSE Scholarship. The Society of Performers, Artists, Athletes and Celebrities for Space Exploration offers two scholarships of $1,000 each. The SPAACSE Galaxy Music Scholarship is available to high school seniors pursuing an interest in space music as a means of expressing the beauty and inspiration of the universe.

Students for Organ Donation Youth Leadership Award. $500 to $1,000 is available to full-time high school students. Students must have made a commitment to raising awareness of organ donation to transplantation.

La Fontaine Aquatic Entomology Award of $500 is available to graduate students conducting a research project in aquatic entomology.

Collegiate Inventors Competition. Applicants must submit an original idea, process or technology that will be judged on originality and inventiveness as well as its potential value to society. The grand prize is $50,000 for the students and $10,000 for the student's advisor.

Illustrators of the Future Contest ($4,000). Applicants must submit three black-and-white works illustrating a science fiction or fantasy story with no recurring theme.

Little People of America Contest. LPA is a non-profit organisation that provides information and support to people of short stature and their families. LPA was founded by Billy Barty, the 3'9" actor who starred in Rumplestiltskin and Willow.

Tall Clubs International (TCI) Scholarship. TCI offers $1,000 scholarships for tall people. Women who are 5'10" and men who are 6'2" are eligible for the award.

New England Chapter of the National Association to Advance Fat Acceptance. The NAAFA offers $500 scholarships for high school seniors who are obese.

National Make It Yourself with Wool Competition. $2,000 and $1,000 for knitting wool garments. Gertrude J. Deppen Scholarships. Available to Bucknell University students who have graduated from Mount Carmel Public High School who are not habitual users of tobacco, intoxicating liquor and narcotics and who do not participate in strenuous athletic interests.

Zolp Scholarships. Restricted to students who are Catholics and whose last name is Zolp. The student's last name must appear on their birth certificate. The scholarship provides full tuition at Loyola University in Chicago for four years.

Patrick Kerr Skateboard Scholarship. One $5,000 and three $1,000 scholarships.

Tupperware Home Parties Scholarship. Available to independent Tupperware dealers, managers, distributors and their dependent children.

Eileen J. Garrett Scholarship ($3,000). For students studying the science of parapsychology.

The Alice McArver Ratchford Scholarship is restricted to females who live on campus, don't own a car, have never been married and who demonstrate financial need.

The Icy Frost Bridge Scholarship at DePauw University is restricted to female music students who can sing or play the national anthem with sincerity.

The Mycological Society of America offers a scholarship of $2,000 for students who are studying mycology (spores, moulds and fungus).

Chick and Sophie Major Memorial Duck Calling Contest. $1,500 to the winner and $500 to the runner-up. The contest is open to any high school senior in the United States who can call ducks. Contestants have 90 seconds to use four calls (hail, feed, comeback and mating).

Vegetarian Resource Group Scholarships. $5,000 for students who have promoted vegetarianism in their schools and communities.

The Western Golf Association sponsors the Charles 'Chick' Evans Jr. Scholarship for golf caddies.

All-American Pie Recipe Contest. First prize of $25,000 scholarship to the Culinary Institute of America.

Eight American colleges currently offer special scholarships and discounts for twins and triplets.

THE 'IG NOBEL PRIZES'

The 'Ig Nobel prizes', presented and honoured by Harvard University, are announced in the same week as the Nobel Prizes. An 'Ig Nobel Prize' is awarded for research at Colleges and Universities that 'cannot or should not be reproduced'.

The 2005 Ig Nobel prize for Peace – and just how it entered this particular category was a mystery to the winners – went to a married couple, Claire Rind and Peter Simmons, for their work at Newcastle University on investigating the brain functions of locusts. These were measured by sitting the insects in front of scenes from Star Wars. The researchers claimed the study had a serious purpose since understanding the brain mechanisms that locusts use to escape predators and avoid collisions may be useful in designing car safety systems.

Edward Cussler and Brian Gettelfinger of the University of Minnesota won the Chemistry prize for an experiment that settled the important question of whether humans can swim faster in water or syrup. The results of this significant piece of research indicated that average speeds in both liquids are about the same.

Victor Benno Meyer-Rochow, of International University, Bremen, won the Fluid Dynamics prize for his paper: 'Pressures produced when penguins pooh: Calculations on avian defecation.' When the birds relieve themselves, they apparently fire a long stream of white faeces from their bottoms. Dr Meyer-Rochow had the enviable task of determining the pressure needed to generate the high speeds involved.

Associate Professor Mike Tyler's team from the University of Adelaide won the Ig Nobel Biology prize for its work on frog smells. Professor Tyler says each frog has a characteristic odour when stressed. 'Most of the tree frogs have odours which resemble either peanuts or cashew nuts,' he said. 'It's very sweet.'

He says another group of frogs have a distinct curry smell. 'In fact, one is a sweet Bombay curry,' he says. 'And there's another one which is more like one of the north Indian chilli-laden curries.' The team have also found about twenty frogs that smell like cut grass but admit, 'there are some rancid ones'.

The researchers are not sure what all the smells mean but have found out that some of the chemicals behind them are responsible for killing mosquitoes. They also found that some chemicals stop pigeons poohing on parapets and are already used as a bird repellent in London, Paris and New York.

A Japanese researcher won the Nutrition prize for photographing and analysing every meal he ate over 34 years.

Gregg A. Miller, of Oak Grove, Missouri, won the Medicine prize for his invention of Neuticles – prosthetic testicles for neutered dogs.

Sometimes the question does arise as to whether the lunatics have actually taken over the asylum or whether we are such a prosperous country that money can be thrown away on the most madcap of enterprises – or perhaps both. Nowhere is this more clearly seen than with contemporary art awards.

In October 2005, the Tate Gallery actually bought a performance work, which does not exist, for the sum of £20,000. 'Time', a creation by David Lamelas, involves asking people to stand in a line and state the time to the person next to them. The money came from the Outset Contemporary Art Fund in which donors give £5,000 towards the cause of buying contemporary art for the Tate. The 'work' was one of a number bought from the Frieze Art Fair in London, which has become the country's largest contemporary art event. Jessica Morgan, curator of contemporary art, spoke of her fascination for Lamelas's exploration of time and said that when the performance piece was staged at the Tate, visitors would be asked to state the time in their own language. 'It's a collective experience. It's relevant for a young generation.'

£15,000 was also spent on a grey filing drawer stuffed with 1,000 blank index-cards, all neatly stacked. The Tate said that the Dutch artist, Stanley Brouwn, deserved greater appreciation for seeing its potential. The same artist's previous works have involved him walking through Amsterdam asking people to draw an arrow on paper to point his way forward. He then displayed the arrows on a table.

Other purchases included two ceiling fans made out of skateboards, colanders and other found objects, and a film showing a performance by a rock band being interrupted by a balloon drifting across the stage. In total, fourteen pieces were bought with a budget of £150,000.

A final thought:

Awards are like piles. Sooner or later, every bum gets one. *(Maureen Lipman)*

14

Facts of Life

Bigamy is having one husband too many. Monogamy is the same.

You've got to be married, haven't you? You can't go through life being happy. *(Colin Crompton)*

The only reason I would take up jogging is so that I could hear heavy breathing again. *(Erma Bombeck)*

Contraceptives should be used on every conceivable occasion. *(Spike Milligan)*

When Lady Astor was canvassing for her first parliamentary seat in Plymouth, a senior naval officer was appointed to accompany her as she went around town knocking on doors. One door was opened by a small girl. 'Is your mother at home?' Lady Astor inquired. 'No,' the child replied, 'but she said if a lady comes with a sailor, they're to use the upstairs room and leave ten bob.'

FACTS OF LIFE FROM THE PRESS

It is strictly forbidden on our Black Forest camping site that people of different sex, for instance men and women, live together in one tent unless they are married with each other for that purpose. The meaning of this regulation is that otherwise the purpose of the furlough, namely, recreation, could not be guaranteed. *(Caravan Club Magazine)*

Mordell Lecture. Professor J. Tits, of the College de France, will deliver the Mordell Lecture at 5 p.m. on Monday, 24 April in the Babbage Lecture Theatre, New Museums Site. The title of the lecture will be 'Rigidity'. *(Cambridge University)*

BRONTE COTTAGE – 17th Century luxury cottage. Ideal honeymoon. Sleeps 2/5. *(The Times)*

Mr E. Brien – In a report last week of a court case involving Mr Edward Brien of Scottes Lane, Dagenham, we wrongly stated that Mr Brien had previously been found guilty of buggery. The charge referred to was, in fact, one of burglary. *(Dagenham Post)*

According to the complaint, Mrs O'Donnell told the court her husband started amusing her three days before the marriage. *(Texas Clarion)*

Sheer stockings, designed for fancy dress, but so serviceable that lots of women wear nothing else. *(Advert)*

Girls for Boys' School – A school for boys, Sexey's School, Lusty Hill, Bruton, Somerset, is to take 22 girl pupils in September. *(The Times)*

She was married in Evansville, Indiana, to Walter Jackson, and to this onion was born three children. *(Ohio Paper)*

Student Derek Sydney Szuilmowski, aged 20, was wearing a skirt, cardigan, underslip, two pairs of tights, panties, and a bra when he sped through Camp Street shortly after midnight, it was stated at Salford. *(Manchester Evening News)*

The new chairman of the South East London Family Planning Association is Mrs Mary Walker, who is expecting a baby in a month's time. *(Croyden Advertiser)*

'Honeymoon? If we can fit it in,' say couple. *(Northern Echo)*

Mounting problems for young couples. *(Western Gazette)*

A study of 13,000 college students found that those given free condoms in giveaway programmes did not engage in more sex than others, and that the notion was unfounded. But they did douse more people with water balloons from their upper-floor dormitory windows. *(From the American Journal of Public Health)*

Miss Giavollela had pleaded guilty to stealing goods worth £25.10 from Tesco Supermarket; to assaulting a policewoman; and to dishonestly handling a garden gnome. *(Oxford Mail)*

Drive carefully in the New Year. Remember nine out of ten people are caused by accidents. *(Falkirk Herald)*

The judge said that when the school organist started to spend a lot of time at the rectory, Mr James warned his wife 'not to get into a position from which it might be difficult to withdraw'. *(Evening Standard)*

Retired teacher Aubrey Westlake is fed up with people asking if his caravan site and holiday centre is a nudist colony; 79-year-old Dr Westlake and his 72-year-old wife, Marjorie, cannot understand what makes people think their 'Sandy Balls Holiday Centre' is for nudists. *(The Sun)*

On Wednesday the 23rd (No Communion Service), the Vicar is conducting a Quiet Day for 40 pupils (recently confirmed) from Brentwood School. The Mothers' Union are catering for their physical needs, which are great. *(Roydon Parish Magazine)*

Your own LOG SAUNA for as little as £650 (plus erection). *(local paper)*

7.25 THE SAINT
Girls! Have you ever wondered what Roger Moore's legs look like? Now is your chance, for in this episode he wears the kilt! And that is not the only thing to watch for. *(TV Times)*

26th October – R.D. Smith has one sewing machine for sale. Phone 46379 after 7 p.m. and ask for Mrs Kelly who lives with him – cheap.

27th October – R.D. Smith informs us he has received several annoying telephone calls because of an incorrect ad in yesterday's paper. It should have read: R.D. Smith has one sewing machine for sale. Cheap. Phone 46379 after 7 p.m. and ask for Mrs Kelly who loves him.

28th October – R.D. Smith. We regret an error in R.D. Smith's classified advertisement yesterday. It should have read: R.D. Smith has one sewing machine for sale. Cheap. Phone 46379 and ask for Mrs Kelly who lives with him after 7 p.m.
(Tanganika Standard)

Mr Charles Narrow, 23, yesterday obtained a divorce from his wife, Sissy, a 16-year-old Sixth Former, on the grounds of extreme cruelty, barely six months after their controversial wedding at a Florida nudist camp. He said she was cold and indifferent after the first three weeks of marriage. The daughter of a nudist camp proprietor, Sissy wore only a veil and a necklace at her wedding. *(News of the World)*

The judge said: 'There was a succession of boyfriends. Each time she would trundle her bed into the kitchen, shut the door and remain there for a substantial time. Then the man would leave and she would trundle the bed back into the bedroom and go to sleep. This must have been extremely embarrassing for her husband. It is possible she just wanted to sit and chat to the boyfriends and took the bed in because of the lack of furniture,' said the judge. *(The Sun)*

No Thanks

So – an American doctor thinks that men of sixty years of age should have two wives, does he? Well, I for one wouldn't want a dirty old man of sixty to share with some other woman - thank you very much!

Mrs N.G. Ewell, Surrey. *(The Sunday Mirror)*

SECRETARY WANTED – Spiritual Healer requires secretary to help cope with large male. Must be good at composing letters. Top salary to right person. *(Psychic News)*

CHEERFUL Lady Companion required in Bath. *(Bath & Wilts. Evening Chronicle)*

Sir,

A few weeks ago, my husband and I went to a party in Neasden, being given by my husband's boss, an insurance broker. The door was opened by the boss's wife, who, much to my husband's astonishment and my shock, wasn't wearing a stitch of clothing. I was embarrassed, distressed and angry, but what can you do when your husband's boss and his wife are involved? I pretended not to notice a thing. *(Men Only)*

Sir,
I am not a Welsh teacher, but I love my country and my language very dearly. Learning Welsh at school did me no harm, as I received equal marks in both languages (full marks). I think that Welsh is far more pleasant and useful than sex, of which many people seem to get so much nowadays. *(Liverpool Daily Post)*

A young Russian man who dressed in women's clothes to sit an exam for his sister was caught by guards suspicious of his 'unusually prominent' bust and heavy make-up, Yasen Zasursky, dean of Moscow State University's journalism faculty, told Interfax news agency. *(Reuters)*

FACTS OF LIFE — GRAFFITI

(On back of unwashed white van)
**Make Love - Not War
See driver for details!**

**My husband's a
marvellous lover
– He knows all my
erroneous zones.**

**Women like the
simpler things
in life – like men**

My sister uses massacre on her eyes

THE ARMY BUILDS MEN
**- PLEASE COULD THEY BUILD ME ONE,
VERONICA?**

**8 out of every 10 men
write with a ball-point pen**
- what do the other 2 do with it?

(Notice in Gents' toilet, Old Trafford)
Please adjust dress before leaving –
I don't wear a dress

Do you have a drink problem? – Yes,
I can't afford it.

Make Love not war - I'm married - I do both

Sex Is Bad For One - **but it's very good for two**

(Road sign)
SOFT SHOULDERS –
but warm thighs

Free Women - **where?**

Support wild life - **vote for an orgy** *(Oxford)*

Sex Appeal - please give generously

**Grow your own dope - plant a man
(On rear window of woman's car)**

15

Would You Believe It?

A miscellaneous collection of things you wouldn't make up . . .

Exam invigilators who noticed that a student in Kuwait City spent a long time looking at his watch discovered that it was equipped with a miniature camera and an e-mail facility so that he could scan questions and send them to friends, who would look up the answers.

A multi-agency project catering for holistic diversionary provision to young people for positive action. *(Luton Education Authority's description of go-karting lessons)*

Men who rang a £1-a-minute sex line to talk to Filipino girls grew wary when the girls used slang such as 'Ey up' and 'Me Duck' and alerted Trading Standards. Andrew Vanderahe, 41, who ran the line, was fined £65 by Nottingham magistrates and told to pay £1,000 costs for describing 40 Nottingham women as Filipinos. *(The Times)*

Notes left for the milkman:
   – Two pints thanks. If this note blows away, please knock.

– Don't leave any milk next door as he is dead until further notice.

– Money on table, wife in bed, please help yourself.

Sign under a clock in a college classroom: 'TIME WILL PASS, WILL YOU?'

'This is a magnificent poem,' said the teacher to the student. 'Did you write it unaided?'

'Yes, sir,' replied the young poet, 'every word of it.'

'Then,' said the teacher, 'allow me to shake the hand of Lord Byron, for I was under the impression that you had died at Missolonghi a good many years ago.'

Could you play Engelbert Humperdinck's 'Please Release Me', because it has sentimental associations for my husband, who hopes to be back with us soon. *(Request – Cleveland Radio)*

Two pushchairs, one cot, changing table, high chair, playpen. Vasectomy sale. Call Lisa. *(In the small ads)*

Little girl: Miss, could you please cut me some fabric?
Teacher: Of course, what width?
Little girl: Scissors, Miss.

At an Oxford College, the main course in Hall was Chilli-con-Carne. The vegetarian option was more mysterious: 'Vegetable-con-Carne'.

MRSA precautions: Sterile nurses – Take patient out of the ward into isolation – Make sure anyone leaving the ward is sterilised. *(Sign in a Nursing School in a hospital)*

Lake Chargoggagoggmanchauggagoggchaubunagungamaugg, Massachusetts.
Translation from the Algonquin: 'You fish on your side of the lake, and I'll fish on my side of the lake, and nobody fishes in the middle.'

Speaker Chris Jolly of the Simplified Spelling Society gavce an interesting talk. *(NUJ Book Branch News)*

Conservatives Have Eyes Riveted To Cabinet *(International Herald Tribune)*

7.30 p.m. INTER COURSE LENT COURSE *(Ippleten village magazine)*

Specialist In Failed Double Glazing *(On the side of a white van)*

RABBI BURNS CELEBRATIONS *(Stevenage Comet)*

THE FINEST IN WALES – English country cottages *(Guardian Classified)*

A monkey trained to pick coconuts jumped on to an almost bald man passing a coconut tree in Kuala Lumpur. He mistook his head for a nut and tried to twist it off. The man was taken to hospital with a strained neck. *(Sunday Mirror)*

Reward for any information concerning a small tan & white short-haired terrier, taken from my yard sometime Tuesday. This dog answers to name of Patches and is very old and stone deaf. 229 Goetting Way. *(Advert in Vista Press, California)*

Miss O'Neill, a former teacher, said Wardlow picked up an axe and struck her twice on the head with it. She was in bed at the time. Shortly afterwards, he hit her with a can of soup. 'He opened it then and we both had the soup,' she said. *(Edinburgh Evening News)*

SOLUTION: If there are two men each of whom marries the mother of the other, and there is a son of each marriage, then each of such sons will be at the same time uncle and nephew of the other. There are other ways in which the relationship may be brought about, but this is the simplest.

In 1983, Prince Charles and Princess Diana visited Australia and New Zealand on a Royal tour. One day on a walkabout in South Australia, Diana headed toward a group of youngsters, the nearest of which she patted affectionately upon the head. 'Why aren't you at school today?' Diana asked. 'I was sent home,' replied the boy, 'because I've got head lice.'

Picasso once fell into an acrimonious conversation with a woman over his so-called art. 'My daughter can paint like that,' she declared at one point. 'Congratulations, Madame,' Picasso replied. 'Your daughter is a genius.'

Have you ever wondered how certain phrases came about?

In 1904, tailors Montague Burton set up a hire shop at which Cheshire men could hire a full suit for special occasions, including a shirt, tie, shoes and socks. They were said to be wearing the 'full Monty'.

Early English doctors believed that a bite wound would heal faster if the hairs of the dog responsible were rubbed into it. Hence the origin of a 'hair of the dog'.

The phrase 'to spill the beans' has its origin in Ancient Greece when new members applied to join a private club. Secret ballots were held using different coloured beans to vote yes or no. These were never known unless someone knocked the pot over and . . . spilled the beans.

'As fit as a fiddle' – in medieval courts the man regarded as the fittest was the fiddler as he danced and pranced around while making his music – somewhere along the line, the 'r' of fiddler disappeared.

Fox lovers in the 1800s would drag cured herrings along the hunting route, away from the position of the fox. The confused dogs would follow the scent of the 'red herring' instead of the fox.

Many centuries ago a man's status was confirmed by the size of the wig he wore – hence 'bigwig'.

Some people just seem to have a gift for spotting trends . . .

I think there is a world market for maybe five computers. *(Thomas Watson, chairman of IBM, 1943)*

I have travelled the length and breadth of this country and talked with the best people, and I can assure you that data processing is a fad that won't last out the year. (*The editor in charge of business books for Prentice Hall, 1957)*

But what is it good for? *(Engineer at the Advanced Computing Systems Division of IBM, 1968, commenting on the microchip)*

There is no reason anyone would want a computer in their home. *(Ken Olson, president, chairman and founder of Digital Equipment Corp., 1977)*

This 'telephone' has too many shortcomings to be seriously considered as a means of communication. The device is inherently of no value to us. *(Western Union internal memo, 1876)*

Who the hell wants to hear actors talk? *(H.M. Warner, Warner Brothers, 1927)*

Heavier-than-air flying machines are impossible. *(Lord Kelvin, president, Royal Society, 1895)*

GRAFFITI

The Mona Lisa Was Framed
(Birmingham)

In people's China the workers take the lead.
(to which was added)
In capitalist England, they also take
the iron, copper, floorboards and the fillings
from your teeth.

(Euston Station)

Thirty-channel TV sets guaranteed working perfect, £50 each - as advertised on Crime Watch
(Oxford Circus)

16

Some Unusual and Amusing Shop Names

Old records and LPs – The Vinyl Resting Place, The Vinyl Frontier, The Vinyl Countdown

General dealers in Edinburgh – Thistle Do Nicely

Estate Agents – Sherlock Homes

Window Dressings – It's Curtains For You

Fish and Chip Shops – Battersea Cod's Home, The Frying Scotsman, A-Salt & Batter-Y, The Codfather

Second World War Memorabilia – Norman D. Landing

Hairdressers – Hair-O-Dyenamix, Lunatic Fringe, Cut Above, Cliptomania

Flower Shops – Sherwood Florist, Open All Flowers

Bread Shop – Knead The Dough Bakery

Perfume Shop – Heaven Scent

Barber Shop – Herr Kutz

Baker's – Slice of Life

Butcher's – Best Joint in Town

Furniture Store – Pining for You , Sofa So Good, Suite Sensation, Suite Success

Beauty Salon – Beauty and the Beach

Off-Licence – The Bitter End

Ladies Underwear – Brief Moments

Bistro – Feast of Eden

Pet Shop – Paws for Thought, Birds of a Feather

Optician – Spex Appeal

Tanning Studio – Tan Tropez

Chinese Takeaway – Wok This Way

Shoe Repairs – Cobblers To You

Gift Shop – Present Company

Funeral Service – Go As You Please *(At this establishment in Whitley Bay, Tyne & Wear, it is possible to be buried at sea for £3,450, and if you are a fanatical Newcastle United supporter you can travel to your maker in a black and white coffin for £250)*

And on the subject of funerals, did you know that?

Lifegem, in Hove, East Sussex, charges between £2,000 and £13,000 for a diamond pendant or ring made from the carbon of human ashes.

Motorcycle Funerals offers a final ride, at £1.10 a mile, in a motorbike and sidecar – one way only.

Space Services, in Houston, Texas, charges £570 per gram for a loved one's ashes to be blasted into space.

Heavens Above Fireworks gives displays of rockets containing cremation ashes. Prices start at £1,500.

Research by Age Concern has shown that people are increasingly opting to be buried with a variety of electronic gadgets and possessions. In 2005, some of the objects which accompanied their owners on the final journey included mobile phones, a fax machine, the remains of pets, cash, golf clubs, a coconut, a bottle of whisky, a can of lager and a packet of crisps, a plant and a personal stereo.

17

Gaffes from TV, Radio and the Press

Spoken Bloopers

The king of verbal cock-ups was Murray Walker as he commentated animatedly and sometimes hysterically through the microphone. Clive James described him thus: 'Murray sounds like a blindfolded man riding a unicycle on the rim of the pit of doom,' adding, 'Even in moments of tranquillity, Murray Walker sounds like a man whose trousers are on fire.' Some of his more hilarious remarks can serve as an introduction to this section . . .

Jensen Button is in the top ten, in eleventh position.

And he's lost both right front tyres.

Mansell can see him in his earphone.

Do my eyes deceive me, or is Senna's Lotus sounding rough?

I know it's a cliché, but you can cut the atmosphere with a cricket bat.

Tambay's hopes, which were nil before, are absolutely zero now.

This has been a great season for Nelson Piquet, as he is now known, and always has been.

And Damon Hill is following . . . Damon Hill.

Jean Alesi is fourth and fifth.

Mansell is slowing down taking it easy. Oh, no he isn't! It's a lap record.

It's lap 26 of 58, which unless I'm very much mistaken is half way.

I was there when I said it.

Of course, he did it voluntarily, but he had to.

Others, besides Murray, became well known for putting their feet in it, and some are worthy of mention, particularly former US Vice President Dan Quayle . . .

If we do not succeed then we run the risk of failure.

I deserve respect for the things I did not do.

The President is leading us out of this recovery.

The US victory in the Gulf War was a stirring victory for the forces of aggression.

The loss of life will be irreplaceable.

And then there are others . . .

Rarely is the question asked: 'Is our children learning?' *(George Bush)*

A zebra does change its spots. *(Al Gore)*

Let's give the terrorists a fair trial and then hang them. *(Senator Gary Hart)*

You can argue about that until the cows come home. *(Environment Minister Elliot Morley in radio debate during foot and mouth outbreak)*

The best cure for insomnia is to get a lot of sleep. *(Senator Hyakawa)*

. . . the wind is shining, and the sun is blowing gently across the fields. *(Ray Laurence)*

I asked the barmaid for a quickie. I was mortified when the man next door to me said, 'It's pronounced "quiche".' *(Italian Ambassador Luigi Amaduzzi)*

An end is in sight to the severe weather shortage. *(Ian McCaskill)*

They couldn't hit an elephant from this dist–. *(Last words of General Segwick in the American Civil War*

Why only twelve disciples? Go out and get thousands. *(Sam Goldwyn)*

Let us toast the queer old Dean. *(Rev. W.A. Spooner)*

Sir, you have tasted two whole worms. *(Rev. W.A. Spooner)*

You will leave Oxford on the next town drain. *(Rev. W.A. Spooner)*

GAFFES AND THE MEDIA

Unless the teachers receive a higher salary increase they may decide to leave their pests. *(Times Educational Supplement)*

Some of the boys' methods are quite ingenious, the professors at the Institute have found. For instance, when asked to multiply 20 by 24 mentally, one gave the answer – 600 – in a few seconds. *(Baltimore Sun)*

It's ten o'clock, Greenwich. Meantime, here is the news. *(Heard on the radio)*

Here's Miller running in to bowl. He's got two short legs and one behind. *(Cricket commentator)*

He's got a great future ahead. But he's missed so much of it. *(Terry Venables)*

And tonight Northern areas can expect incest and rain – er, sorry about that, incessant rain. *(Radio weather presenter)*

Remember the name – it's big Seven and U-P after.' *(Radio advert)*

Fiona May only lost out on the gold medal because Niurka Montalvo jumped further than she did. *(David Coleman)*

Do you believe David Trimble will stick to his guns on decommissioning? *(Radio One Newsbeat)*

It was the fastest-ever swim over that distance on American soil. *(Interviewer, UTV)*

Despite fears that the balloon may be forced to ditch in the Pacific, Mr Branson remains buoyant and hopes to reach America. *(Portsmouth News)*

It has been the German Army's largest peacetime operation since World War 2. *(Radio 5 Live)*

Do Britain's drug laws need a shot in the arm? *(CNN News)*

Police and Customs officers retrieved a cannabis haul today in a joint operation. *(Radio Cleveland)*

Ian Mackie is here to prove his back injury is behind him. *(Radio 4)*

And that was played by the Lindsay String Quartet ... or, at least, two thirds of them. *(Template Times)*

HEADLINES WITH A DIFFERENCE

THE LIFE OF HORATIO NELSON – For details see top of column *(Radio Times)*

MAD COW TALKS *(Huddersfield Daily Examiner)*

NOTHING SUCKS LIKE AN ELECTROLUX *(Used by the Scandinavian vacuum manufacturer in an American advertising campaign)*

COUNCIL STAMPS ON DOG'S MESS *(Leighton Observer)*

SURVIVOR OF SIAMESE TWINS JOINS PARENTS *(Boston Globe)*

IRAQ HEAD SEEKS ARMS *(Sydney Mercury)*

EYE DROPS OFF SHELF *(Medical News Magazine)*

JUVENILE COURT TO TRY SHOOTING DEFENDANT *(Court News)*

STOLEN PAINTING FOUND BY TREE *(Slalom Post)*

TWO SISTERS RE-UNITED AFTER 18 YEARS ON CHECK-OUT COUNTER *(Financial Mail)*

RESIDENTS FLEA IN ARSON ATTACK *(Worthing Herald)*

CARLESS DRIVING CASE IS ADJOURNED *(Scarborough Evening News)*

PROSTITUTES APPEAL TO THE POPE

COUPLE SLAIN. POLICE SUSPECT HOMICIDE

CONMEN PRAYING ON VULNERABLE PEOPLE

PANDA MATING FAILS: VET TAKES OVER

ASTRONAUT TAKES BLAME FOR GAS IN SPACE

KIDS MAKE NUTRITIOUS SNACKS

SOMETHING WENT WRONG IN JET CRASH

COLD WAVE LINKED TO TEMPERATURES

LOCAL HIGH SCHOOL DROPOUTS CUT IN HALF

TYPHOON RIPS THROUGH CEMETERY – THOUSANDS DEAD

TWO SOVIET SHIPS COLLIDE – ONE DIES

LUNG CANCER IN WOMEN MUSHROOMS

SCHOOLBUS PASSENGERS SHOULD HAVE BEEN BELTED

POLICE CAMPAIGN TO RUN DOWN JAY-WALKERS

TROOPS WATCH ORANGE MARCH

CHEF THROWS HEART INTO FEEDING NEEDY FAMILIES

BRITISH UNION FINDS DWARFS (sic) IN SHORT SUPPLY

POLICE SUBDUED MAN WITH CARVING KNIFE

STEALS CLOCK, FACES TIME

PASSENGERS HIT BY CANCELLED TRAINS

POLICE FOUND DRUNK IN SHOP WINDOW

NEW SHOCKS ON ELECTRICITY BILLS

POLICE SAY DETECTIVE SHOT MAN WITH KNIFE

PRESSMEN GATHER TO SEE ROYALS HUNG AT WINDSOR

CATERING COLLEGE HEAD COOKED FOR THE QUEEN

MAN IN THAMES HAD A DRINK PROBLEM

COUNCIL DECIDE TO MAKE SAFE DANGER SPOTS

FIREMEN TO SHOW THEIR APPLIANCES TO PASSERS-BY TO ATTRACT RECRUITS

CHAMBERMAID HAD POT

FARMER'S EIGHT-HOUR VIGIL IN BOG

PEER'S SEAT BURNS ALL NIGHT – ANCIENT PILE DESTROYED

SAVAGE APPOINTED HIGH COURT JUDGE

SHELL FOUND ON BEACH

FILMING IN CEMETERY ANGERS RESIDENTS

NO WATER – SO FIREMEN IMPROVISED

PRISONERS ESCAPE AFTER EXECUTION

ANTIQUE DEALER THOUGHT GIRL WAS OLDER

GAS RIG MEN GRILLED BY VILLAGERS

STAR'S BROKEN LEG HITS BOX OFFICE

QUEEN SEES FONTEYN TAKE 10 CURTAINS

SPOTTED MAN WANTED FOR QUESTIONING

SPARE OUR TREES – THEY BREAK WIND

And getting it right below the headlines can be a tricky business, too!

On making enquiries at the hospital this afternoon, we learn that the deceased is as well as can be expected. *(Jersey Evening Post)*

A woman mourner was horrified when her best hat was buried with the coffin at a South African funeral – she had planned to wear it to a cocktail party later the same day but an undertaker mistook it for a floral tribute. *(Weekend)*

The bride was attended by two bridesmaids. Both were nearly attired in dresses of fawn georgette. *(Lincolnshire paper)*

The landlord insisted that no female should be allowed in the bra without a man. *(Glasgow Herald)*

ROY ROGERS – Roy Rogers, 66, singing cowboy star of many films and television westerns, was in a 'stable condition' yesterday after undergoing open-heart surgery at Torrance, near Los Angeles. *(Daily Telegraph)*

Bulmers achieved its position after a programme to improve conditions for its 1,000-strong Hereford workforce, which have included profit-sharing, annual bonuses and a 35-day week. *(Hereford News)*

Responsible preventative measures such as neutering need to be taken very seriously by car owners. *(York Evening Press)*

The Canine Defence League also offers a low cost neutering service to pensioners and people on means-tested benefits. *(West Briton)*

Have you got the longest legs in the East Midlands? Pretty Polly has announced that gorgeous and glamorous Tania Strecker is the new face of Pretty Polly Nylons, modelling its recently re-launched bestselling hosiery range with her amazing 37 legs. *(Long Eaton Trader)*

Correction: Hakin girl wins lap dancing certificate. The headline should have read: Hakin girl wins tap dancing certificate. *(Milford & West Wales Mercury)*

Many people were dubious about the prospect of a large metal deer in the park, fearing it could turn into a white elephant. *(Ealing Gazette)*

The Institute Management Committee held its monthly meeting in the committee room. Alan Day, chairman, showed samples of carpet, which will be used in the ladies toilets and carried through the reading rooms. *(Westmorland Gazette)*

Brigadier Chris Sextor unveiled the plague with officials. *(KM Extra)*

The toilets were in a terrible state, they hadn't had a penny spent on them since the sixties. *(Manchester Metro News)*

The Women's Institute will hold their fortnightly lecture in St Mary's Hall, the topic will be 'Country Life' when Mrs Wills will show slides of some beautiful wild pants. *(Matlock Mercury)*

Personally, I would welcome a plague dedicated to Bill Owen because he was a fine actor . . . *(Huddersfield Daily Examiner)*

At a meeting to discuss the route of a proposed ring road, the highways committee chairman said: 'We intend to take the road through the cemetery – provided we can get permission from the various bodies concerned.' *(West London Observer)*

I was so pleased to read that the city councillors rejected plans to turn Worcester Angel Mall into a café brassiere. *(Worcester Evening News)*

Notices/Signs/Announcements/Small Ads/Labels

IN CASE OF FIRE, PLEASE DO YOUR UTMOST TO ALARM THE SCHOOL CARETAKER *(School notice)*

The typists' reproduction equipment is not to be interfered with without the prior permisssion of the office manager. *(On school staff-room notice board)*

Staff should empty the teapot and then stand upside down on the tea tray *(Staff-room notice board)*

Afterwards mice pies and wine will be served and anyone wishing to sing a song will be welcome. *(Halifax Evening Courier)*

MEXICAN NIGHT – Complimentary Punch On Arrival *(Promotional flyer)*

Join us in the drawing room for a pre-dinner drink. Pour over the menu and place your order. *(Time-share brochure)*

... currently have vacancy for the following: Brassiere Supervisor *(Wigan Reporter)*

Bring Me Sunshine – Male, 55, 5'10", enjoys bawling, dancing, socialising, seeks female for friendship. *(Northampton Evening Telegraph)*

Genital male, lonely 35, single dad, 5ft 10, dark hair, brown eyes, seeks female, for friendship and romance. *(Towcester Post)*

Experienced Au Pair Girl, experienced in housework. Especially enjoys cooing. *(Evening Standard)*

BOX of mixed body parts, suitable car boot. *(Alton Gazette)*

Retired lady seeks modern gent, 60–70, must be non-smoker with a good sense of humour, honest, loving and reliable, to enjoy each other's company, must be impotent. *(Louth Target)*

Deep freeze meat: best Scotch meat from Wales. *(Edinburgh Evening News)*

1990s LARGE pram, with rain cover, sun canopy and mattress, ideal for grandparents, £20. *(South Wales Evening Post)*

CAN YOU LOSE 15LB BETWEEN NOW AND CHRIST-MAS? YES! Natural products, follow-up service. Phone Christ on . . . *(Boston Standard)*

LOST – Lost at the Coigach Gathering, a stainless steel vacuum flask. Used for collecting veterinary faeces samples. May have been mistaken for hot drinks flask. *(Ullapool News)*

(This sign from Plevna, Montana where a letter has fallen off)

PLEVNA PUB IC SCHOOL

Are you fit and healthy? Do you enjoy working with people? Yes? Then we need you, FULL or PART TIME. Both positions are on a shit roster.

PART-TIME PEOPLE – required to fill sandwiches.

Please write your name in the log. *(At the entrance to the local sewage works)*

A police crackdown on credit fraud has been given a major boost after a detective forged vital links with American banks. *(Kentish Times)*

NESTING BIRDS – YOU MUST NOT GO BEYOND THIS NOTICE *(Farne Islands – National Trust)*

PLEASE GO AWAY *(Sign in window of a travel agency)*

BARGAIN BASEMENT UPSTAIRS *(In a London department store)*

WE DISPENSE WITH ACCURACY *(Notice in a Sunderland chemist)*

PLEASE BE SAFE – Do not stand, sit, climb or lean on the zoo's fences. If you fall the animals could eat you and that could make them sick. Thank you. *(Notice in American zoo)*

SLUG PELLETS & AUNT KILLERS FOR SALE

Patrons are requested to remain seated throughout the entire performance. *(Sign in theatre near the public toilets)*

The contents are sufficient for a pie for six persons or twelve small tarts. *(Label on jar of mince)*

Everlasting love, guaranteed to last for five days. *(Label on Valentine bouquets)*

Widows made to order. Send your specifications. *(Ely Standard)*

Need urgent funds. In return will walk around London dressed as a giraffe for a week. *(Camden News)*

Our's are the happiest hour's in town. *(Outside a restaurant at Great Park in Ruberry)*

Crisis as hospital opens with skeleton staff *(Nairobi Times)*

NICKI McKENZIE – Congratulations. You never cease to fail us. Lots of love, Mum, Joe, Ang., Mut. Your are very special: Brad *(Coventry Evening Telegraph)*

UNWANTED Christmas present – Jazz CD (Barry Tyler's original Dixieland Jazz Band) and pair of incontinence pants, both hardly used. *(Royston Crow)*

Owing to circumstances beyond our control the previous list published last week has been changed to the dates given below. We apologise for any incontinence caused. *(Crawley Horticultural Society)*

FREE NEUTERING – Cats Protection is offering to neuter your car for free. *(Newbury Weekly News)*

20 toilet rolls, hardly used, Xmas bargain, £3.50. *(Barrow-in-Furness Evening Mail)*

To touch these wires is instant death. Anyone found doing so will be prosecuted. *(On sign at railway station)*

Do not use orally after using rectally. *(On instructions for electrical thermometer)*

Do not sit under coconut trees. *(On a West Palm beach)*

These rows reserved for parents with children. *(In a church)*

Prescriptions cannot be filled by phone. *(In a clinic)*

Keyboard not present – press any key to continue. *(Error message during boot-up on computer)*

THE BEST OF PRODUCT WARNINGS

Caution: The contents of this bottle should not be fed to fish. *(On a bottle of dog shampoo)*

For external use only *(On a curling iron)*

Warning: This product can burn eyes. *(Also on a curling iron)*

Do not use in the shower. *(On a hair dryer)*

Do not use while sleeping or unconscious. *(On a hand-held massaging device)*

Shin pads cannot protect any part of the body they do not cover. *(On cyclists' shin guards)*

This product not intended for use as a dental drill. *(On an electric rotary tool)*

Do not drive with sunshield in place. *(On a car sunshield)*

Do not use near fire, flame or sparks. *(On an 'Aim-n-Flame' fire lighter)*

Do not eat toner. *(On toner for printer)*

Do not use orally. *(On a toilet-bowl cleaning brush)*

Keep out of children. *(On a butcher's knife)*

Not suitable for children aged 36 months or less. *(On a birthday card for a one-year-old)*

Do not use for drying pets. *(In a microwave manual)*

For use on animals only. *(On an electric cattle prod)*

For use by trained personnel only. *(On a can of air freshener)*

Keep out of reach of children and teenagers. *(Also on a can of air freshener)*

Do not use as earplugs. *(On a pack of silly putty)*

Warning: Has been found to cause cancer in laboratory mice. *(On a box of rat poison)*

Remove infant before folding for storage. *(On a portable walker)*

Do not iron clothes on body. *(On the package for a Rowenta iron)*

For indoor or outdoor use only. *(On the package for Christmas lights)*

Wearing of this garment does not enable you to fly. *(On a child's Superman costume)*

Flies coming into contact with this preparation of DDT die without hope of recovery. *(on the bottle's label)*

Do not use while sleeping. *(On a Sears hairdryer)*

Fits One Head. *(On the box of a hotel-provided shower cap)*